FINDINGAMANFORSYLVIA

ISBN 13: 978-0692406632

ISBN: 0692406638

Published in the United States of America

Editor, Rory Olsen

Cover design and interior layout, Steven Lesh

StoryRhyme.com Publishing, 2nd edition (March 1, 2015)

To Steve and Melinda,
who wanted more of Julia's story,
this is for you.

Chapter One

There's something I need to get off my chest, a confession: I am a terrible matchmaker. Everyone knows this. But there's this belief I have, way down to my core, that every one of us deserves love—the good, the bad, the warty; the well-meaning types who choose to wear ugly holiday sweaters with appliques; even the tall and gorgeous, like me. We're all equal in the eyes of love. Or we should be, in a perfect world.

John Donne wrote his famous quote: "No man is an island," and it took a while—years, in fact—for me to actually get what he meant. Maybe I'm not the sharpest knife in the drawer, but it was one of those things that never really made sense to me until one day, I was walking down the street, feeling anxious at the sight of an old man shuffling along, clutching his cane. I watched him wobble alone with no one to mind him. What if he were to fall as he crossed the street? Who would catch him and bandage his wounds? Where was his *wife*?

It hit me then, as I watched the old man walk, what Donne meant. Human beings were not meant to wander this earth unloved and unattended. We're not *supposed* to live wretched lives of desperation and misery. This is why I decided to find a man for Sylvia.

Javier warned me, in no uncertain terms, against it.

As I lay in his arms one night in bed, shortly after first meeting Sylvia, and stated my intentions, he said to me, in a very serious voice, "Babe, you don't get to mess with the neighbors."

This was a problem seeing as how I'd already taken out my mental Rolodex and was flipping through it.

So I tried reasoning with him.

"Jav, it's okay. I have the perfect—"

"No." He shook his sexy bald head, emphasizing his point. "No. We've been through this before. You're a terrible matchmaker. Remember?"

"What do you mean, 'remember'? You're asking me to agree to a fact when there's been no proof of that fact's existence." Sometimes I get all legal on Javier, thanks to the job I had working in a law office that summer from hell.

Javier's face took on a pained expression, and he got the patronizing tone in his voice where he draws out his syllables in an annoying way as if I've suddenly become incapable of understanding simple words.

"*Okaaay*, you want to play it that *waaay*? Remember Chris? Ring any bells? *Hmmm*?"

Of course I remembered Chris. Chris is my brother. That was when I broke away from Mr. Smarty-Pants and rolled over onto my side of the bed with my back to him in protest.

"But I *really* thought he and Michael would hit it off," I said to the wall with a bit of a whine.

It was lame; I knew this. But I'm not one to admit defeat easily. My stubbornness is only outweighed by my sheer adorability.

"Why would two people with nothing in common hit it off?" he asked, pressing his point.

Javier was right, of course. Chris listened to Gregorian chants; Michael liked hitting the clubs. And leather. It wasn't a successful match. And neither one spoke to me for at least two weeks afterward. But sometimes you have to be willing to take a little heat when you're a warrior for love.

Wait. Did I just say that?

There had been other unfortunate matchups. Fiona and Francesca, for instance, my lesbian friends, who threatened to boycott me after a disastrous blind date arranged by yours truly. Then there was my best friend Lisa and most of Javier's friends, two of his employees, and my auto mechanic Billy Bob. But Lisa is like catnip to men. They're initially drawn to her, but when the temporary high wears off, they have a tendency to crash hard, and the recovery period varies depending on their length of exposure. But Lisa is a special case and not necessarily a good measure of my matchmaking capabilities.

Javier says God laughs at me and my good intentions, and we *all* know what the road to Hell is rumored to be paved with. But I have one simple question for Javier: How does he know God's not laughing *with* me?

Chapter Two

I first met Sylvia when she moved into the neighborhood two years ago, directly across the street from me. The tired little Spanish-style bungalow had been vacant for months, its previous owners victims of LA's post-Great Recession dog-dropping economy.

The movers had been there all morning, and I'd been working in our front yard, pruning roses, playing with my daughter Matilda, throwing a stick for Dave the dog, waiting for a glimpse of the new people. As I pulled dandelions out of the little strip of lawn between the sidewalk and the curb, a gray Oldsmobile pulled up. I watched as a slight woman in her thirties got out and took a large box out of the trunk. She added a smaller one on top, and yet an even smaller box on top of that, struggling to balance the three.

I sprinted across the street, eager to offer help, not stopping first to wipe the dirt from my hands, as she fought for control.

"Hey, do you need a hand?" I called from just behind her. She jumped, causing the box on top to teeter. I tried to grab it, thrusting my body over to catch it but instead collided with her elbow, which made her lose balance all together. I felt helpless as the box fell to the ground. The sound of shattering glass gave me a slightly sick feeling. It was clear that whatever was inside the box was now pulverized.

Crap.

"Sorry," I said, with a weak smile. I picked up the small box and held it up to my ear, shaking it a little. The remnants made a tinkling sound. My only explanation for this is nervous energy. Other than that, I have no idea. "Oh, no. I'm so sorry," I apologized again when I realized what I'd done. Clumsy.

"That was my grandmother's teapot," she said, in a quiet voice. "I think the china factory was bombed during World War II." She said this almost offhandedly, with knitted eyebrows.

Again, crap.

Our eyes met over the now-dented box as I gently set it back on top of the two larger boxes she was still holding. The look on her face was the same look that my daughter Matilda gets when she realizes I've eaten the last Ding Dong, forlorn and wistful.

"So I'm guessing I won't be able to buy a replacement?" I offered.

"No, I guess not," she said with a frown.

There was no point in lying and passing myself off as the Avon lady, especially since I still had dirt under my fingernails and was wearing one of Javier's old T-shirts, so I decided to come clean and introduce myself.

"I live across the street," I said, gesturing to our house, the light pink bungalow with longish grass and trash barrels still sitting out in front of the curb, lonely and forgotten. "Um, we've been so busy this week; we haven't had time to do the yard yet."

It was a lie, and I don't know why I bothered since she was bound to catch on to our lax gardening habits once she'd been around for a while, but I guess I was hoping to at least give her the *illusion* that we were responsible. Javier is an artist and doesn't view the world in absolutes of manicured lawns and clean driveways. He has more of an abstract yard aesthetic. Me? I'm lazy. Something about her, though, made me feel that I needed to explain myself; I felt self-conscious and gawky, as if I were in the sixth grade again, all long legs, arms, and pre-braces overbite.

She sighed and shifted the large box onto her hip. "It's all right. We have a lot of old stuff."

I followed her to the front door, volunteering helpful pieces of information, such as, "Trash pickup is on Wednesdays." She glanced back over to our trash bins; her eyebrows had the knitted-together look again. "And the mail usually comes around eleven."

Silence isn't something I'm comfortable with; I want to fill it, so I tried to keep the conversation going. And I wondered about the old stuff to which she had made reference. Was it extra emotional baggage? Or did she mean it in the literal sense as in they were a family of hoarders? Which could be totally interesting and disturbing at the same time.

She went inside and set the boxes down on the floor of an Art Deco-style kitchen. Following behind, I leaned a shoulder against the kitchen's arched doorway. I'd never been inside the house since the prior occupants were odd ducks. The husband had once told me that he worked from home as a screenwriter. The only times I ever saw him, he was wearing flannel pajama bottoms and an old T-shirt, and that was at four in the afternoon. The wife worked the night shift at the state prison. They weren't the friendliest people in the world. Once in a while, we'd exchange uneasy waves, but that was the extent of our interactions with one another.

I glanced around the kitchen. The floor's black-and-white ceramic tiles were laid out in a checkerboard pattern, and the countertop was lined with little yellow tiles. It was charming and lovely.

"This is a great little kitchen. I love the tile work," I said as Sylvia started opening cupboards. She was taking inventory, even though the kitchen had nothing to inventory.

"My mother's happy with it," she said with a shrug, continuing to open and close doors, familiarizing herself with her surroundings.

When I'm confused about something, Javier says I cock my head to the side, kind of like that Internet video of the adorable bulldog puppies who all turn their heads at the same time in the same direction giving them this mechanized effect as if they're little robot dogs. Sylvia waited for me to say something.

"How old are your kids?" I asked.

She paused, holding on to one of the lower cabinet doors, peering inside at the darkness.

"Kids? I don't have any kids."

It was strange because Doris, the neighborhood news source, had mentioned in passing that the new owners had kids, and I'd been looking forward to a new playmate for Matilda.

"Oh, I thought—it doesn't matter. I'll let you get back to unpacking."

"I live with my parents and older brother."

"Oh."

She laughed bitterly. "Yeah, I know. It sounds like I'm a loser when I say it like that."

"Oh, not at all. Don't be silly," I said, patting her on the shoulder. Of course, I was lying again. One adult child living at home with their parents was interesting; two was a syndrome.

"Wait. I didn't mean to be rude," she said, taking a moment to stop and give me her full attention. "I'm Sylvia. I didn't catch your name."

I hadn't given her my name, which may have been my subconscious mind wishing to remain anonymous, as if she'd forget all about this awkward encounter, and we could start fresh next time. She held her hand out to me as we stood in front of the empty space where the refrigerator would go. Her hand was soft and delicate, and in that split second as I held it, her life story flashed through my mind. As I looked into her sad brown eyes, I saw a quiet girl who'd kept her hand down in class; I saw lonely days and nights. I *felt* the poignancy of a hungry soul longing for contact. That island thing again.

In Sylvia's face, I saw a woman who'd never really been kissed by a man. I'm talking a *real* kiss with heat and passion; a kiss that leaves a person gasping for breath, wanting more; a kiss felt down to the soles of the feet. An all-over, body-tingling kiss

10

with hands exploring. His hands. Hers. Bodies entwined. Soft and sweaty. Heart pounding. A kiss with all or any of the preceding, but, hopefully, all.

In that moment, I felt supremely bummed.

It's strange, but sometimes I can be very perceptive about things. Almost extra perceptive. Like, for instance, I can tell if a person's got a good heart, or if they're a complete ass. I can tell if they're strictly an upscale, fine-dining type of person, or if they'd be happy sitting around in flip-flops drinking a beer and swapping embarrassing stories about high school. I get *feelings*. In that briefest of moments as I looked into Sylvia's eyes, I knew her story.

"Oh, sorry. I'm Julia Florez," I said, still holding her hand, suddenly aware that she was trying to pull hers away.

"That was interesting," she said, with a surprised laugh when I finally let go of her hand.

"I know," I said. "Did you feel it too?"

She had a little frown on her face now as if she thought I was a complete psycho nut.

"Uh, I think I need to get back to unpacking."

It wasn't going as well as I'd hoped.

"Sorry," I apologized again. "I can be a little too much sometimes. I can get a little overly enthusiastic with the handshakes."

"Florez?" she said, looking at my blond hair and white skin.

"Hawthorne-Florez," I said, nodding. "It was really good to meet you, Sylvia. I'll see you around. Let me know if you need anything. And welcome to the neighborhood."

"Thanks," she said, holding a piece of teapot in her hand. It was the handle, I think.

Now, *that* hurt a little.

Chapter Three

On a fall Saturday afternoon which held the unwelcome promise of endless five-year-old coed soccer games, almost a year to the day after I'd had the unhappy encounter with Sylvia's teapot, Javier took pity on me, taking over as soccer dad, leaving my afternoon open. It was cool and crisp out—the perfect day for sitting around talking with a friend who I hoped to get to know better. After numerous invitations on my part and mumbled excuses on hers, I'd finally managed to pin her down.

We'd been getting to know each other, the two of us, gradually stripping away the layers as you do with a new friendship. My layers were stripped away up front because I'm a classic over-sharer. Sylvia's were worn away more gradually.

We sat at my little kitchen table drinking and talking about the elusive nature of love, which, after three margaritas, naturally led to tears—Sylvia's in this case.

She tapped her fingers on the red Formica surface of our 1950s era table and chairs set and sighed.

"I don't know. Somewhere I just gave up. I realized love wasn't going to happen for me. Ever."

"Oh, come on. That's not true."

She made a face. "Please. Maybe not for you. Look at you. You're gorgeous."

It's true. I am. And I've never had self-esteem issues, which is probably one of the reasons I've never had trouble attracting men. My problem was always more of a *choices* thing, as the life coaches of the world might say. That is, making very bad choices in men and having the tendency to pick the ones who were less like men and more like fourteen-year-olds with attention deficit disorder.

"Look, Sylvia. I've kissed a *lot* of frogs."

"Oh?" she said, now interested. "How many frogs?"

"Okay, let's not get into the numbers. We're talking about *you* now. You're a beautiful woman."

"Oh, no." She was shaking her head, one of those people who don't know how to be complimented.

"No," she continued, a wistful tone to her voice, "I've resigned myself to spending the rest of my life living with my parents. I'll be a spinster like my Tia Maria."

"Who's Tia Maria?" I asked.

"My mother's sister." Sylvia sighed. "She's never been married. She still lives with my grandmother."

I shuddered at the thought of a lifetime stuck at home with the parents. Don't get me wrong, my parents are, and have always been, great, but the whole situation was unnatural and seemed very much like living the life of a martyr. I felt suddenly depressed.

"So why didn't she ever marry?" I asked.

"I'm not sure. There was an old family story about her parents not approving of the man she loved and chasing him off." Sylvia gave a snort. "I've never had *that* problem. I mean, not having ever had a man for my parents *to* run off."

She added the last part, I guess, just in case I was a total idiot and needed clarification. I put a few more crackers out on the cheese plate and offered her one. The mood at the kitchen table had grown morose, but only for a moment. My wheels were turning—and that's *usually* a good thing.

"Have you thought of contact lenses? Or a little eyebrow shaping? You've got a great natural arch. They need a little neatening is all." Or hedge trimmers to cut through her near monobrow, but I couldn't tell *her* that.

There were things I knew we could do to get her into shape, and I was mentally making her over, taking notes in my head, carefully looking at one side of her face, then the other. So far, she was sending a message to the world that said: I'm not interested, *and* I don't want to get to know you.

I was hit with a sudden revelation. "You've got a heart-shaped face. Do you know how many women would *kill* for that?"

She brought a hand up to her forehead, feeling it and hiccuping. "Excuse me."

"And you've got great hair," I continued, "if you'd just get rid of those stray grays. Pluck a little here and there, a little lipstick, liner, mascara. Fabulous." I snapped my fingers for emphasis.

I pulled her glasses away from her face, touching her chin, turning her face one way, then the other, as she sat there blinking her eyes, trying to focus.

"Sylvia, I don't get it. What the heck is your problem? You have a beautiful face. Why have you been hiding yourself away?"

She dabbed a few pieces of salt off the rim of her glass with her finger and licked it, then leaned her head back to get the dregs of margarita mixed with crushed ice stuck to the bottom. She gave her glass a few quick taps, and the entire mass came loose at once, sloshing onto her face, spilling all over the ugly sweater she was wearing.

"Oops," she said, and giggled.

I wasn't sorry to see the ugly white sweater covered in strawberry margarita; it deserved to die.

"Here," I said, handing her a kitchen towel. She grunted and made a couple of halfhearted attempts to dab herself before reaching for the pitcher, refilling her glass and breaking into a few heaving, miserable sighs, head in hand. It was only four-thirty in the afternoon, and she was already a complete mess.

"I hoped one day a man would materialize out of thin air, I guess," she confided. "Just like that. You know how you have those fantasies of the perfect life?"

I nodded. I did. It's what we all dream about—what we have forced down our throats almost from birth. Fairy tales and princes. Grand expectations. Castles in the sky. I knew the whole bit.

"He'd stop and notice me, give me a little smile." She sniffed, wiping her nose indelicately with the sleeve of her ugly sweater. "Maybe we'd talk about the weather, maybe there would be a suggestion of coffee."

She had it all planned out. I listened to her, with my head resting on my hand, as she told me how her Prince Charming scenario would work.

"Every day at work when I go to lunch, I sit on the same bench in the park. It's ridiculous, I know," she said, now laughing at herself. At least she'd stopped crying.

"Have you thought of trying a new bench?" I asked. She snorted again.

"Funny."

"Sorry."

She went on to describe how for years, she'd taken her lunch break out in the open, exposing herself to the world; how, optimistically, she'd nibble her chicken salad on wheat and the uniformly cut carrot sticks her mother Ofelia had prepared with love that same morning.

"And every morning, she recites the following prayer over every slice of bread: 'Blessed Virgin, please send a man for my daughter.'"

I interrupted her sad monologue. "Dude, does your mother really pray over your sandwiches?"

This was met with an eye roll.

"My mother prays over everything. By the time she's done with my lunch and Raul's, she's made a whole trip around her Rosary beads."

I resisted the impulse to comment on the sheer ridiculousness of her seventy-five-year-old mother still making her lunch. If she didn't get it—well, there were limits to my powers.

The problem with Sylvia's sad lunchtime tableau for one was that most of the men at the park were either homeless guys or old grandfathers running their little photo businesses where they'd offer posed Polaroid pictures in front of a backdrop of the Hollywood sign for ten dollars apiece, holdovers from the pre-digital camera age.

"There was one man. He worked at the legal document place next door."

Her eyes misted over as she thought about him for a second.

"And?" I leaned over, interested to hear about her mystery man.

She paused, glass in one hand, self-consciously playing with her long, black hair, wrapping sections around and around her fingers as she thought about Legal Document Guy.

"And…what?" I urged her on. "Details!"

She sighed.

"He came into the bakery one day for an empanada. I was working in my office, but there's a little window that looks out into the front. He was so handsome. He reminded me of Ricky Martin."

"Mmm, Ricky." I sighed.

"I was too nervous to go out and talk to him though. He bought his food and left. And each day, I waited for him."

I pictured the handsome stranger, feeling myself getting all starry-eyed thinking about the two of them together.

"After two months of waiting for him to notice me, one day, as I sat there on my bench in the park nibbling my little carrot stick, he walked up. His eyes met mine. He smiled. Right at me. His teeth were *perfect*."

I was on the edge of my seat; my pulse quickened.

"I was so nervous, and I sat on my bench trying to think of something to say. I was getting all ready—"

"And?" I interrupted, leaning forward on the edge of my chair.

"And then I saw the beautiful woman he was really looking at. It wasn't me. I could have been the bench, for all he knew."

I slumped in my chair.

"He put his hand on her waist and kissed her. I might as well have been a fat stupid pigeon," she said, disgusted with herself. And a little harsh, to be honest.

The sun sank lower in the sky, I found another shirt for her to wear, and we refilled our glasses. Sylvia counted on her fingers for me, reciting the different boys and men who'd made up her string of anonymous crushes.

"There was Freddy. He played the oboe—he was very intense—in eighth grade. We were just friends. Then James my freshman, sophomore, *and* junior years of high school. He was my biology lab partner. We were just friends."

I was beginning to notice a pattern.

"Then football player Mike half of my senior year." She sighed a dreamy sigh.

"Don't tell me; you were just friends?"

"Oh, no. Mike didn't even know who I was."

"Ah."

"There was Mr. Casal at City College, my art teacher. He was a short and wore a fedora to class every day. He wasn't much to look at," she said philosophically, "but he had a way of commanding the room. And he was mysterious."

"Well, he sounds interesting," I volunteered.

Sylvia was quite depressed now, with her head hanging down.

"Did you ever try to become *more* than friends with any of them?" I asked. "Did any of them ever know how you felt?"

She shook her head. "I can't. I'm too shy. It's my curse."

We stared at each other across the table; for once I was at a loss for words.

"Legal Document Guy was three years ago. That's when I decided, right then and there, to give up on men."

"That's it? Three years ago and nothing?" I was stunned by her admission. The thought of living without a mate was so foreign to me. Completely unacceptable. It was like hearing one day that chocolate in all forms had been banned. No *way*. Sylvia was letting fear rule her life; it wasn't right.

She looked at the table, into her drink, at her fingernails, then back into her drink.

"Well," she said tentatively, "there is someone else."

Her eyes had a desperate, half-crazed look now, possibly from the tequila.

"Who? Who?" I implored.

"You sound like an owl."

"You can't just leave me hanging here." I was starting to get a little exasperated with my quiet friend.

"His name is Tom."

I pounced. "Okay? And? Details, please."

"Wait." She held up her hand as if she were about to swear an oath. "Father Tom."

This was the part of the afternoon where I found myself with a gaping mouth as I tried to focus on this particularly important yet improbable piece of information. Sylvia pushed her chunky black glasses higher on her nose, then wiped a little bit of drool away from her mouth with her sleeve, again, rather inelegantly.

Now, we were both, admittedly, three sheets to the wind, but I had the feeling that my friend had just admitted to being in love with a Roman Catholic priest. Serious no-no time. Unless he was willing to turn in his collar, there was no way anything good could come of this situation. *And* knowing Sylvia and her past history, he was more of an excuse, a safe bet—not someone she had any real hope of a relationship with.

"Do *not* go all *Thorn Birds* on me now," I warned her.

"Seriously. I love him. I love Father Tom. His curly brown hair, his blue eyes, his strong hands…" She hiccupped once and was gone. Her brain had floated off to another place, thinking about her priest in shining armor.

I wanted to reach over, grab her by her collar and shake her, yelling, "Wake the eff up!" but I restrained myself, saying this instead:

"Dude, your mother would shit. Then she would fall over and die. Right there on the spot. Do you really want your mother to die?"

Her eyes were half-closed now as she started to rock back and forth a little, moaning, "I know, I know." She sat up and looked me in the eye. "And stop calling me 'dude.'"

"I can't help it. I grew up at the beach."

And I did. "Dude" was something we called everyone from the mail guy to my elementary school principal, Mr. Cox. And it was better than calling him "Mr. Cox."

I was curious; I had to ask.

"Why are you in love with him? What is it about him that's got you so hung up?"

It occurred to me that possibly something had happened between the two of them, some interaction or innocent flirtation. Or maybe not so innocent—like maybe they'd hooked up? It was a long shot, but being the thorough investigative type (i.e., nosy), I thought it imperative to try to get to the bottom of the situation.

Sylvia looked at me with mournful puppy eyes. "There's no reason, other than the fact that he's perfect in every possible way. He's handsome and kind and gentle…" And she was off in her fantasy world. I swore under my breath. She looked up at me— hope in her eyes.

"Wait. Isn't your brother a priest?" she asked with a sudden burst of energy.

"Yes. He's also gay. Wrong church though. He's an Episcopal priest, which means he can have a girlfriend or a boyfriend or get married and adopt an orphan from the Third World, if he wants."

Sylvia's face brightened for a second as she contemplated Father Tom converting from the Roman church to the Church of England.

"Couldn't he become an Episcopal priest too? I mean, couldn't he?"

She tried to convince me as I shook my head silently.

"It's possible. And there's this bridge I have for sale. I can sell it to you right now, if you want, for a very reasonable price."

"I hate you," she said softly.

I nodded. "I know, I know. Love hurts. But—" I held a finger up in the air for emphasis "—there's always hope."

"Hope," she murmured quietly and repeated it as if it were her new drunken mantra. "Hope, hope, hope," she slurred, rocking back and forth in her seat.

My new friend was now half-past drunk, and, truthfully, looked terrible. I had the distinct feeling that she wasn't the experienced drinker that I was.

What are we going to do with you, Ms. Sylvia?

The headlights from Javier's VW shone through the kitchen window as I poured the dregs of the margarita pitcher into the sink and started the coffee pot. It was time for some serious strategizing on my part. And sobering up on Sylvia's.

Chapter Four

The morning after Sylvia's margarita-fueled confessions, I did something I'm not very proud of. It may possibly have been a personal low point, even for me. I stalked a priest. I stalked a man of the cloth—someone whose life is devoted to all things God. As I said, I'm not proud of this, but then again, there are very few things I've done in life that I am truly proud of besides marrying Javier and giving birth to my daughter.

I got up early. Too early. My hangover was slight; the bags under my eyes were not.

Javier lay in bed snoring rhythmically, sounding a little like a gas-powered chainsaw. He stirred, coughed once, scratched his backside, opened his eyes, looked at me, and said, "Babe, what are you doing?"

I was getting into my skirt, pulling it over the mountainous hip region.

"I'm going to Mass."

"It's not Christmas," he said simply before rolling over.

"I know. I'll be back in an hour. If Matilda wakes up, fix her a bowl of cereal."

This was unlikely. The earliest Sunday Mass was at seven-fifteen a.m.; I knew the Cruzes didn't usually go until the nine-fifteen service. Matilda would easily sleep for another hour.

My husband snorted and resumed his regularly scheduled program of snoring. I tucked my hair behind my ears, put on a little lipstick, foundation over the blemishes, liner, and was out of the house in five minutes.

St. Mary's is the not-so-little church around the corner. It's an older Gothic-style dark, scary, foreboding Wuthering Heights-ish type of place. I've been there for the usual baptisms and first communions, and it always leaves me feeling a bit small, judged, and unworthy.

As I sat in a middle pew and waited for the service to start, I studied the stained glass windows depicting the saints in their various states of martyrdom. Unwittingly, I'd picked a spot next to the window showing the Prophet Isaiah being fed a burning ember of coal by a heavenly angel swathed in light and white robes. St. Mary's is not the kind of place a person wants to go when they're feeling all insecure about life, God, and other things. I tried to formulate a prayer as I knelt down on the worn padded kneeler. My knees felt all knobby and uncomfortable.

God, I know it's been a while. Please forgive me for stalking Father Tom. It's just, my friend, Sylvia. She really needs a man. I'm not saying it should be Father Tom or anything like that. I mean, I know he's taken already. I guess, just maybe if you could think about sending someone nice. A good guy. Thanks, God. Oh, right. It's me. Julia.

My prayers are a little shaky since I'm not a regular person who prays, but the preceding is an approximation of what I asked for in the moments before the service started.

As I got back up on the hard wooden pew and sat down, rubbing my knees, a very old woman took the seat next to me. Her head was covered by a black lace veil. She gave me a disapproving look as if she knew I was there for inauthentic purposes. I disliked her for being so judgmental and toyed with the idea of making a face at her, but the altar boys and their fresh, innocent faces stopped me in the nick of time.

The full set of players processed up the aisle, and I searched for Father Tom. I spotted him as he followed a much older priest carrying the Missal. The older man, with his full head of white hair and puffy red face, reminded me of the kindly-looking mall Santa Claus we'd taken Matilda to see last Christmas. But Father Tom? I got it. I really did. He was hot. Smoking hot. It was a wonder the pews weren't full of women throwing their underwear at him. He was a dead ringer for Colin Farrell, and I felt slightly unhinged by his overt handsomeness. It didn't seem right. Father Tom's dark hair, long eyelashes, and smiling face in conjunction with his priest's collar seemed to be a cruel joke played out on all womankind.

I'd seen enough and mumbled an apology to the mean old woman as I stumbled out of St. Mary's and into the bright sunlight somewhere around seven-twenty a.m.

I admit, I may have cut out of the service before it really got started, but I learned something very important from my ten minutes on the inside: I knew what Sylvia liked—handsome, unavailable men. This little bit of information I hoped would serve me well in my matchmaking search, even if I was going to Hell.

I arrived back home to find Matilda parked in front of the television with Dave lying at her feet as usual. Javier was sitting next to her on the couch attempting to focus. They were watching the Disney channel. Javier's eyes narrowed suspiciously when he caught a glimpse of me.

"What are you doing home so early? I thought you went to Mass."

He has a way of asking the most annoying pointed questions.

"Oh, I just wanted to say a few prayers, light a candle."

"For who?"

"For whom," I corrected. Anything to shut him up. My head was beginning to throb a little from the drink the night before. And lying takes concentration—concentration I felt myself lacking at that moment. "Tillie," I asked my daughter, "want a Pop-Tart?"

"Pop-Tart? That's not a *real* breakfast," Javier said, with a large amount of scorn.

Maybe I'm not Mother of the Year. In my defense, my head was seriously pounding at this point. Besides I knew the suggestion of a Pop-Tart would not fly. I have my ways of getting Javier to cook. And I was right. Within minutes, the smell of chorizo and scrambled eggs filled the kitchen.

Javier is smart. He knows there are few things in life I find more erotic than him cooking—chopping onions, beating eggs, shredding cheese, and warming tortillas. Some of our best make-out sessions have begun after, or during, a meal he's prepared.

We sat in the living room around the television balancing plates on our laps. I felt his eyes on me as I ate.

"So are you going to tell me what's going on?"

"Javier. Let's talk later," I said, with a nod toward Matilda who didn't need to hear adult conversation. It's handy having a kid nearby sometimes to diffuse unwanted conversational subject matter.

"She's not paying attention," he said.

Matilda was focused on her cartoons and ignored our mysterious adult conversation, pausing intermittently to interrupt us with her string of free-association non sequiturs.

"Danielle's mom makes waffles for breakfast."

"Oh, that's nice," I said.

Thirty seconds later, face still turned to the television: "Olivia's getting a puppy."

"Good for Olivia," Javier said.

Eyes still focused on the program. A few seconds later. "I like puppies. Can we get a puppy for Dave to play with? He's lonely."

"No. One dog is enough," Javier said before turning his attention back to me with an expectant look on his face. His gaze remained fixed on me.

"Can't talk. Eating," I mumbled, shoving half a corn tortilla in my mouth.

"I'm waiting," he said, drumming his fingers against his knee.

"All right." I put my plate down on the coffee table. "I went to church because I wanted to check out Father Tom."

Javier's eyebrows were raised, confused. "Why?"

"Because Sylvia's in love with him."

Javier shook his head. "Ay, yi, yi."

"I know, right?"

"That's a shame—" he shook his head sympathetically "— but what does *this* have to do with *you*?"

He seemed to be suspicious that something else was really going on. He's very sharp, my husband.

"Okay," I said, deciding to come clean with him. "Javier, you know how I feel about lonely people, right?"

He stared and nodded patiently; I continued.

"Because Sylvia's so *desperately* in love with Father Tom, I wanted to see, take some notes."

My husband remained silent, staring at me impassively. He is one tough audience. I cleared my throat and took an extra breath for courage. "I've decided. I'm *going* to find the perfect match for her. It's a *quest*," I said with extra feeling, so he'd know not to screw with me.

He scooped the rest of the eggs and sausage up with a tortilla and finished eating in silence.

"So we're good here?" I asked the stone face.

He wiped his mouth with his napkin before addressing me.

"Babe, you know how I feel about your matchmaking. We've been over this. I'm going to have to forbid it."

I couldn't help it; I started to laugh. His use of the word "forbid" made him sound like a tyrant with an eye patch and heavy black gloves out of one of those old war movies. I could picture him making a fist with one hand and pounding it into the other hand for emphasis, forbidding me from doing things. "*I forbid you to work outside of the home. I forbid you from wearing pants.*" It was ridiculous. His forbidding might have worked if we were somehow able to get into our time machine and travel back in time about five hundred years or so. My outburst was not welcomed; I could tell by the way he glared at me, so I decided to humor him.

"Okay, Master. I will leave her alone."

He raised a skeptical brow. I got up, bowed once, and took the dishes into the kitchen.

Matilda had been humming a catchy little TV commercial jingle about hamsters, and I heard her ask Javier, "Daddy, can we get a Hello Kitty waffle maker?"

Five-year-olds are adorable. I felt all sunny and warm inside as I loaded the dishwasher and schemed, ignoring my husband's proclamation.

Javier. He can be adorable too; he just doesn't know it.

Chapter Five

Javier and I stood in line at Juanita's on Soto, the little hole-in-the-wall place where we order our Thanksgiving and Christmas tamales. The smell of cinnamon from the Mexican hot chocolate was thick in the air. The woman behind the counter wore a hairnet under her cap and had an extra pencil tucked behind her ear. She scribbled furiously on a sketchpad, trying to keep the line to a manageable length, when Javier gave me some unexpected news.

"Babe, I was looking at the calendar for the new year. This year, Cinco de Mayo falls on a Saturday!"

He was happy, practically bouncing up and down like a little kid who's about to receive his first two-wheeled bike.

This was *big* news in our world. Javier's Cinco de Mayo parties were legendary in our circle of friends, family, casual acquaintances, and everyone else that happened to be within a five-mile radius of our house. In fact, his annual blowout was where we'd met seven years before. I was twenty-nine and young for my age (i.e., immature), and he was a much more mature (i.e., together), older man of thirty-one.

I remember that night well—the walk up to the little bachelor-sized back house, past scores of motorcycles, glancing around at the unfamiliar surroundings, feeling slightly off balance.

"It looks like a Harley Davidson convention," I said to my oldest friend who'd heard about Javier's little soiree from God knows where. Lisa wasn't the most reliable source when it came to parties, but I tried to keep an open mind.

"Don't look at *me*," she said, giving her bra strap a little tug and pulling at her too-tight miniskirt. "I'm liking what I'm seeing so far though."

She was scanning the men—the prospects—deciding who to focus her energies on.

"Hold me back," she said, her voice a low rumble. The object of her lust was a man with thick strong arms and a black muscle T-shirt. "See ya later." She gave a little wave and a wink and was off to the hunt, leaving me behind. I cursed her first, and then cursed myself for letting myself be talked into going with her. Again.

Lisa runs through men. I'm not saying she's a whore *exactly* because her behavior is the same behavior men have been getting away with for centuries. But she'd left me at a complete stranger's party, somewhere between the curb and the backyard, to fend for myself. She'd left me so fast, in fact, it made my head spin.

I made my way down the long uneven driveway leading to the back house, passing girls in short dresses and guys in jeans, white T-shirts, and bandannas. It was all very much like a high school party but with old people.

As I stood in line at the keg, cursing my friend's treachery, Javier approached. One look at his bald head, goatee, and neatly trimmed mustache, and I was hooked.

"Here. Let me get that for you," he said, taking the red plastic cup from my hand and filling it, handing it back to me with a soft smile. Our eyes met as our hands touched. A spark passed between us. I'd heard about "the spark" but had never experienced it in real life. Not like that.

"I'm Javier. This is my house. Welcome."

Our eyes were locked, having their own conversation. In his eyes, I saw my future. I'm not sure what he saw in mine, but I'm pretty sure it involved me being naked.

"Hi, Javier. I'm Julia, your new girlfriend."

He laughed, raising a brow. "Do you live around here?"

"Yeah, I'm just over in Echo Park. I live with my friend Lisa, who…just dumped me."

He was nodding his head, smiling. "I like her already."

"Cheers, Javier," I said as we clicked plastic.

We chatted; he refilled my cup, ignoring the people around us.

"Come with me," he said, taking me by the hand. The spark again. It was like a charge of energy coursing through my body; even my toes tingled. I had the most intense desire to jump him; it was strange. He took me to a spare corner of backyard behind the garage, passing party guests—a group disproportionately made up of drunken bikers—looked into my eyes and asked, "Do you mind if I kiss you?"

It was so nice that he asked first, and unexpected. There had been *so many* frogs, I'd lost count.

"I'd mind if you *didn't* kiss me," I answered, turning my mouth up to meet his.

And then he kissed me. I practically heard The Crystals singing their song about the wonder of new love. It was like The Wall of Sound in the background. It was heat and passion—our own new symphony. But it wasn't *all* lust and animal attraction. Trite as it may sound, we connected that night on an emotional level, the same way any two people in the world who'd experienced too many lonely nights would.

We stayed up all night talking, and when the sun rose and he told me, "I will love you for the rest of my life" in a voice choked with emotion, it wasn't weird or obsessive, because I felt the same way. He held me close, his lips brushing the top of my head, and I repeated his words back to him, "I will love you for the rest of my life."

Sometimes life is like that. Sometimes things *are* that simple.

Javier opened up to me that first night, telling me about growing up with his single father, Frank, and his younger brother.

"She left one day when I was in third grade. Dad found a note. That was it. They were so young when they had me, still in high school." His face was more wistful than sad when he told me about his mother. "I forgave her a long time ago though."

I touched the side of his face, murmuring, "I'm so sorry. That must have been so hard for you."

He kissed me again, and it was soft. Magic.

I cheered him up, making him laugh with my stories about my parents and their hands-free approach to parenting and its obvious effects on me. Their laissez-faire approach had at least worked with one of us. I'm not sure where they went wrong with Chris though.

We made love and laughed some more, and it felt like I'd known him for all of my life.

We were married the next Cinco de Mayo, which—magically—fell on a Saturday, one year to the day from our first kiss. We've been together, more or less happy, ever since—except when I'm confounding his sense of propriety and decorum with my uncontrollable periodic urge to match people.

I don't really know how to explain in a rational manner what happened between us to bring us together that night, but when Matilda was born on that very holiday the next year, arriving two weeks early, Javier took this as a positive sign that her birth date was preordained by God. *And* that he should continue to hold his rager parties.

In the five years since her miraculously timed birth, we've hosted combination Cinco de Mayo/birthday parties. The fact that both events would once again land on a Saturday—well, this meant the attendee list and celebration could be kicked up a few notches. Or more.

I returned back to Earth after my visit to memory lane and gave him an enthusiastic nod.

"Great, babe. We'll start planning immediately."

"Oh, I'm way ahead of you," he said, rubbing his hands together, smiling to himself—smiling on the inside, smiling on the outside. I wanted to squeeze him tight and hug him for being so openly excited about such a thing as a holiday, but since we were in Juanita's shop surrounded by children and old people, I reached over and gave him a discreet peck on the cheek, squeezing his arm instead.

"Congratulations," I said with as much enthusiasm as I could muster in the stuffy, crowded shop.

It hit me then as we waited in line: I had six months, give or take a couple weeks, to find a man for Sylvia.

The man? He was unknown to me, but he *could* be one of the guests. It would be a perfectly natural place for her to meet the man of her dreams, and *so* easy for me to slip someone in under my suspicious husband's radar.

Hey, the magic of Cinco de Mayo had worked for me. Couldn't it work for her too?

Chapter Six

I'd been considering the options and coming up short. The loneliest man I knew was Ken, our mail carrier. How did I know he was lonely? It probably had something to do with his hungry eyes, and the way he'd stare at me on Saturdays when I'd work outside in the yard. But I scratched him off my mental checklist, because there's this distinct *feeling* I get from him and his hungry eyes that he really just wants to keep me in his basement. Normal is fairly important. In fact, it may rank higher than looks in my matchmaker's checklist.

There were Javier's silkscreen shop employees to consider, but that didn't take long. Jimmy, at twenty-six, was energetic and handsome, but there *was* that little grand theft auto incident when he was young and careless, and his subsequent prison stay. I could just picture Sylvia's father Antonio going after him with a pitchfork. *That* probably wouldn't go over too well.

Robert, Javier's press operator, was a giant of a man. He rarely spoke, and when he did, it was to demand food, mainly Big Macs, which Javier would inevitably run out and get for him, because Javier knows that a press operator is worth his weight in gold, and Big Macs, apparently. He was kind of scary and foreboding, though, so I crossed Robert off the list. The only other worker in Jav's shop was George, but he was married with three small children.

What to do? The strains of soft workplace disco played in the background as I drummed my pen along with the beat against my desk at work. The day before Thanksgiving was always slow, especially in the medical equipment rental business. As a result, my job filling orders was finished well before noon.

Acme Medical Supply is perhaps the world's most boring company. I work there because I am a college dropout and my options are severely limited due to my inability to stay with any job longer than two weeks during my wild, impetuous youth. Also, I thought the name Acme was meant to be ironic in a Wile E. Coyote-on-rocket-skates kind of way. As it turned out, I was wrong. The owner simply wanted his company's name to be listed first on the building's directory sign. My disappointment is only tempered by the necessity of paying the mortgage, so I suck it up and die just a little every day.

As I sat shuffling through lunch menus, Ted, the office accountant, passed by, avoiding eye contact as usual. Ted was kind of an odd bird, prone to nervousness, especially when conversing with a woman. His face was buried in a spreadsheet. The blue-and-green argyle sweater he wore was quite fetching, so I complimented him on it.

"Hi, Ted. Looking good today. Great sweater."

"Uh, hi, Julia. Thanks. Uh, is that a new blouse?"

It was cute, his awkward attempt at conversation, as if he knew it was the correct social thing to do but wasn't skilled enough to know just how to go about it.

"This old thing?" I said with a laugh then immediately wished I hadn't. The look on his face was one of discomfort. "How's Lord Byron?" I asked, hoping to deflect his embarrassment. Lord Byron was his overweight tabby with an apparent eating disorder. The greedy kitty had a tendency to binge and purge, causing Ted an endless amount of consternation and stress. The only time Ted ever left work early was because he had to take Lord Byron to the vet again as a result of him either going off his cat food or throwing up all over Ted's apartment.

"He's been having a little bit of a rough go lately," he said, frowning.

"Oh, I'm sorry. Indigestion?"

"Something like that."

Ted was not what you'd call an over-sharer. He doled out bits and pieces of his life as if they were precious treasure. Information was strictly on a need-to-know basis. A bit of a mystery to me, he also happened to be good-looking, with a thick head of curly, dirty-blond hair and the most beautiful green eyes. He could have been a spokesmodel for Bausch & Lomb.

Through dogged persistence, I'd managed to accumulate a fair amount of information about Ted Wilson in the three years since he'd been employed at Acme. For instance, I knew he was thirty-two years old, lived alone, had no known health problems but was prone to seasonal allergies and occasional bouts of asthma when the pollen count got too high. It's remarkable, the information one can learn when they have access to a person's confidential personnel file.

He didn't appear to be gay, but I wasn't one hundred percent certain about this, and I was fairly positive he wasn't a serial killer. Items spotted in his cubicle included assorted books of poetry, an old-style fountain pen complete with nibs, and a French-to-English dictionary, so I knew he was a sensitive, thinking type. Also, he liked to work Sudoku puzzles during his breaks. When pressed for time, he was prone to eating microwaved Cup O' Noodles or a quick Hot Pocket. So his taste in food was definitely not as good as his taste in clothing. But nobody's perfect.

What stood out about Ted to me, more than anything else, was that he seemed to be living a life of quiet desperation. I knew this from hearing his side of the conversation when he was speaking to his mother on the phone, massaging his temples, looking as if he wanted to commit hari-kari.

To his extreme annoyance, Ted's mother, Bitsy, called frequently and at least once a month tried to set him up with one of her friends' daughters. A typical Ted and Bitsy conversation would go something like this:

"No, Mother. Absolutely not. I can't. I'm busy. And you *know* I can't stand Phyllis. Why would I want to meet her daughter?"

Their conversations would invariably end with him cutting the conversation short by feigning a sudden work emergency or meeting. Poor Bitsy was afraid she'd die grandchildren-less.

Ted stood awkwardly before me, lamenting his poor dumb fat kitty, and I felt a sudden twinge of inspiration. What could be more perfect and beautiful than bringing two shadow people together? It was the *exact* right thing to do. Ted and Sylvia were both background players. Who could *possibly* be a better match for my love-worn friend? I was practically picking out their china pattern, wondering what their children would look like. Good-looking, of course; very shy.

"So, Ted, what are you doing for Thanksgiving?" I said, making conversation, trying to draw him out a little.

He began to fumble and stammer, "Oh, Thanksgiving. Um, wow. I hadn't—I—uh…"

Only Ted. He hadn't a clue, and it was the next day.

"We're eating at three. Join us. Please. I insist."

"Oh, uh, my mother—"

"Is she trying to set you up again?" I said with a laugh, teasing him just a little. His parents lived back home in Salt Lake City, and it was just like Bitsy to have arranged a space for him at some eligible young lady's parents' dinner table for the holiday.

He was looking down at his shoes; I leaned over from my seat at the reception desk where I was temporarily filling in and looked down at them too. They were brown brogue oxfords, the type serious professionals and college professors wear. His coordinated blue-and-green argyle socks were hot in an "I'm in love with my teacher" sort of way.

"Really, I insist. No one should be alone on Thanksgiving."

I immediately regretted saying that. Nobody wants to feel like they're unloved and unpopular. No one wants to feel like a lonely loser. I hoped he didn't feel that way from my offhand remark, but he looked at me, right in my eyes, and nodded.

"That sounds nice. I'll be there."

"Fabulous."

He took a few steps and then stopped, turned and asked, "Red or white wine?"

"Both," I answered, surprising him. I was only half joking.

As he walked back to his cubicle, I had to stop myself from rubbing my hands together like Snidely Whiplash, whom I didn't resemble in this context at all. I was using my powers for good. This time.

Chapter Seven

Since I've been known to burn water, ruin hard-boiled eggs, and use my own oven as storage back when I lived the uncomplicated life of a single girl, I've been banished from most kitchen activities. And *what* could be the downside of this, I ask?

I have my gifts though, like excellent table-setting skills. And I can put together one hell of a centerpiece using items found in the yard—autumn leaves, halves of shells, and those little tiny pinecone-looking things I've never know the proper name of. But there is no fear in this situation. Javier is a great cook. Growing up with his overburdened single dad and a little brother to take care of, he'd spent countless hours in the kitchen with his Abuela Terry. She taught him how to make delicious cocido—a savory soup with big hunks of beef, zucchini, carrots, potatoes, and little cobs of corn—or they'd prepare homemade salsas and delicious marinades for carne asada.

Little Javier would stand by Terry's side in the kitchen, using a step stool and wearing a dish towel tied around his waist for an apron. Terry gave him important lessons on proper chopping technique and what spices go best with what food. He soaked the information up like a sponge.

Lucky, lucky me.

My husband knows how to cook; I know how to eat. And there is *nothing* quite as sexy as the sight of him on Thanksgiving Day in his snug white T-shirt, first patting the turkey dry, and then lovingly rubbing its skin with olive oil, pepper, salt, paprika, and garlic. I find the whole process strangely erotic.

I watched him work, rubbing and patting, and fought the urge to rip his shirt off so I could rub my face in his chest hairs. Instead, I hung around like a pesky gnat buzzing in his ear, nibbling his shoulder.

"Mmmm, that looks good, babe," I said, nuzzling his neck.

"Get away, woman. Out of my kitchen."

"There's nothing you can do about it," I teased him. His hands were full of olive oil. He couldn't make me do anything.

"Almost ready with the bread crumbs?" he asked, in an obvious attempt to get me to focus my attention elsewhere.

"Ah, I knew there was something I forgot."

"Julia!" he scolded me, impatient. "I'm ready for them now. *Andele!*"

"Give me five minutes," I promised, cursing my attention deficits under my breath, and rushed to find Matilda whose help I could enlist. What are little kids for if not those pesky household tasks?

Matilda sat next to me on the couch, with Dave at our feet acting as our footrest, strategically positioned for maximum crumb retrieval. We watched the Macy's Thanksgiving Day Parade, and I soon found myself distracted by her new game of ripping the bread into different shapes.

"Look, Mommy! This one's a star."

She held the piece of mangled bread up proudly. I didn't "get" the star, but I am a keen booster of the arts.

"Good, Tillie. It's the perfect abstraction of a star. In fact, it really looks like a star in its last stages before it becomes a supernova and explodes."

Her eyes were wide. "Whoa," was all she was able to manage. "Now I'm going to make a heart."

She really is adorable.

"Where's my stuffing?" Javier bellowed from the kitchen. He trends toward the grouchy side of things when he's pressed for time, especially knowing a houseful of people will be depending upon him for their annual meal of thanks and gratitude. We were expecting the usual suspects: my parents and brother, Chris; Javier's dad, Frank; his little brother Rudy and family; Grandma Terry; Lisa, the dominatrix; and last, but not least, Ted.

Our house was always open to those with nowhere to go. When I'd mentioned the night before that Ted would be joining us for dinner, Javier was completely unfazed by this news.

"Great. We'll put another chair around the table." He stopped, thought for a second, and added, "Are you sure we won't be too much for him?"

"Oh, Javier. Don't worry. We don't bite. Well, Lisa does, but she's the only one. I just won't sit them next to each other."

Javier's eyebrows were knitted together in thought. "Hmm. Think about it. Your parents. Lisa. My dad. Our characters are real characters, you know?"

I did know. I was well aware of the fact that we all can be a teensy bit of personality overload.

"Well, Jav, it's either eat here with us, be with the fun crowd, or spend the day with some boring family he doesn't know at all who want to set him up with their daughter. Where would you rather be?"

Javier nodded. "Good point." He snapped his fingers. "Actually, I just thought of something."

"Oh? What's that?"

My interest was piqued.

"We'll get him drunk."

That Javier. He's always thinking. It sounded like a solid plan to me.

"I'll make the bed in the spare room," I volunteered. The thought of drunk Ted was appealing. I'd never seen him outside of his natural work environment, and I really wanted to see what made him tick. There *had* to be more to him than the quiet, sensitive wallflower persona he revealed to the world. And, truthfully, I needed to get to know him a little better so I could plot my matchmaking strategy.

There I was, standing in our bedroom, rubbing my hands together again as Javier shot me a puzzled look.

"Julia, is there something I need to know?" he asked, just a little suspicious.

"Nope. Nothing. Nothing at all."

He shook his head, muttering something about "My wife…" and "…feel like I'm living in an *I Love Lucy* episode."

Oh, Javier. He had no idea.

There are few places more interesting than our dinner table during one of our mixed family get-togethers. Newcomers tend to have a variety of reactions. Either they cautiously sit back and listen, they jump into the fray, or they fall somewhere in between the two extremes.

I'd been playing around with the seating arrangement and decided to put Ted between my brother Chris, the priest, and Frank. Javier's father is a little loud sometimes and rough around the edges, but he's almost always fun. And a little scary. But more fun than scary.

With all three extra leaves in the dining table, we had enough room for everyone, even a section for Matilda and her cousins down at the end where they'd be far enough away to be out of earshot of our adult conversation. A G-rated conversation at this gathering was mostly out of the question.

Javier was pulling the turkey out of the oven when I heard the doorbell ring. It was three on the dot.

"It must be Ted, babe. He's very punctual."

"Well, I hope he's not hungry. He may have to wait awhile with this group," Javier said as he maneuvered the large bird onto a pile of newspapers that had been placed on the countertop to be used as a large trivet.

"Hmm, I'll see what I can do to entertain him."

It could be a challenge, entertaining Ted, but I was up to the task. I smoothed my blouse and checked the entryway mirror to make sure I didn't have any lipstick on my teeth and opened the door to Ted. He was decked out in all of his preppie glory and reminded me of the dreamy tux guy in that old board game Mystery Date. "Will your date be a dream or a dud?" Thinking back, I should have known my brother Chris was gay when we'd play together and he'd wish for his dream date, handsome tux guy, who happened to also be *my* dream date.

Even in his fetching wool sport coat and tie, perfect teeth, hair, and long, dark lashes, Ted remained self-conscious, but he had the wine, so at least his priorities were in the right place.

"Ted, it's so good to see you. Come in."

We both went in for a hug at the same time. I held my cheek out for him to kiss, but our timing was off, and we ended up kissing wrong, and the wine bottles he was holding got in the way, and it felt just the *tiniest* bit awkward.

"Uh, am I early?" he asked, looking around at the empty living room as I ushered him inside. I gave my little "it's-nothing" laugh that Javier says sounds like two martini glasses clinking together at a party.

"Oh, Ted, I'm sorry. I should have mentioned Hawthorne-Florez time. On time is *actually* twenty minutes late. *Late* is showing up an hour after the designated start time. What you *really* want to do is shoot for thirty to thirty-five minutes past to really get in with the crowd."

"Um, is there anything I can do?" he asked, standing in the middle of the room holding the wine bottles, looking a little desperate.

"Well, the living room rug could really use a run-through with the vacuum."

He shot me a surprised glance. "Uh, okay." He handed me the wine bottles then began to remove his jacket.

"Oh, Ted, I'm just messing with you. Have a seat. I'll get you a drink."

I'd started to take the wine into the kitchen when Dave burst in through the dog door having finally realized there was company, which meant a new rear to sniff. I had no idea what he'd been up to in the backyard, but his snout was covered in dirt, and he made a beeline for poor Ted who sat uncomfortably on the couch, eyebrows raised at the sight of Dave barreling toward him.

"Dave! No!" I barked.

Dave is not a very good listener. Strands of slobber and pieces of dirt were now covering poor Ted's slacks.

"Dammit, Dave, you big bastard!" I let loose on the poor dog as Matilda came running from her bedroom to see what the commotion was all about.

"It's okay. Really. I like dogs," he said, brushing himself off, not looking at all like he was really *that* fond of dogs. Ted was a cat person through and through, and he now seemed a bit scared of me after my outburst. I set the wine bottles down, knelt over and nuzzled Dave's face. "I'm sorry, you big baby," I said to show Ted I wasn't a complete monster.

"Matilda, this is our friend Ted. Why don't you get your Chutes and Ladders game. It's Ted's favorite." I gave Ted a little wink. "I'll be right back."

Two minutes later, I handed Ted his first glass of wine of the day, a California Merlot, and a very healthy pour at that.

"Uh, thanks. Let me just get in a seated position here," he said as he got down on his hands and knees, folding his body into a cross-legged position across the rug from Matilda. "I've never played this one. You'll have to tell me how."

She began to explain the rules of the game to Ted, Chutes and Ladders novice. I really wonder about him sometimes, like did his parents keep him locked away in the basement while he was growing up? His lack of knowledge of the most basic things was troubling.

"Mommy, there are no people!"

Matilda was looking up at me with alarm.

Shoot. We'd taken the little cardboard people playing pieces out when she wanted little tiny dolls for her cousin Blanca's dollhouse. And we never got them back.

"They're in Blanca's dollhouse, Tillie."

Her arms were now folded in silent protest. Ted reached into his pocket, pulling out a handful of change. "Um, here. You can use a nickel, and I'll use a penny. How's that?"

Matilda shot me a look of pure skepticism. For a five-year-old, she can be fairly judgmental.

"Have fun, you two! There's the door," I lied, rushing over to answer the door, knowing there was no one on the other side. I knew my chances were at least fairly good, though, that someone would be walking up, since it was now a quarter after three, and we still had a dozen guests yet to show. The porch was empty, so I sat down on the wooden bench outside and waited.

It felt good sitting for a moment, enjoying the cool fall air and the smells of sage stuffing. I knew Javier would soon be calling me to help him, and the running to and from the kitchen would be endless.

My break was short-lived. My father-in-law, Frank, was coming up the walk followed close behind by Lisa, who was, as is her normal practice, wearing a very short leather skirt and tight blouse.

Nice Thanksgiving ensemble, Lisa. I could always count on my old friend to keep things interesting.

Frank wore his usual and customary uniform of pressed blue jeans, crisp white T-shirt, red flannel shirt over that, and matching red bandanna tied around his long, graying black hair. I watched as Lisa, wearing five-inch heels, struggled to catch up to Frank who seemed to be actively avoiding her. There was something about the two of them that had given me the strongest sensation over the years that they had *some* kind of history together, but I'd never been able to pin either one of them down about the subject. It remained one of life's unsolved mysteries. Still, I made sure the two of them weren't sitting next to each other.

Who knew entertaining could be so fraught with social intricacies?

Frank kissed me on the cheek, saying in his low sexy voice, "Julia, when are you going to run away with me?"

"The second Javier gets a beer belly, I'm outta here."

We laughed. The two of us always flirted with each other. For an older man, Frank is very handsome. And he *could* very conceivably be someone I could see myself going out with if I weren't already with Javier. He's fifty-four and works out regularly, has a good head of hair, and is still quite the ladies' man, *which* also happens to be his biggest problem. He's unlucky in love. Correction. He's been lucky over and over, just not with the right woman. His most recent live-in arrangement ended badly with his much-too-young-for-him girlfriend Jennifer attacking him in the parking lot of a biker bar with a spike heel in one hand and a vacuum cleaner cord in the other. The whole scene had been pretty ugly, from what I heard. I don't know what action on his part precipitated the parking-lot attack. For once, I didn't want to know details.

Frank went inside to greet Matilda, while Lisa gave me her typical greeting.

"Anyone interesting I should know about?" My body froze for a second; I wanted to kick myself. "Hmm?" she purred in her innocent black widow way.

I realized I'd made the most amateur of all rookie mistakes: I'd provided fresh prey for this cold-blooded huntress. We walked in together as Frank said hello to Ted and Matilda.

"No," I said emphatically. "There's *no one* here for you."

She stopped in her long-legged tracks when she saw Ted, jabbing me in the side sharply.

Noooooo! My world was beginning to spin out of control.

I grabbed her arm, again insisting, "Don't even *think* about it. He's off-limits."

She shook me off and was within an inch of Ted in less than a second, she's that good.

"Hello," she said with her hand extended, "I'm Lisa." She practically oozed warm and fuzzy. Black widows can be very deceptive when they wish.

Ted's cheeks were crimson, and I cursed silently. His blush was just the sort of thing to set Lisa's predatory heart aflutter. She has a particular fondness for virgins, which I'm guessing Ted was. The hamster wheel in my head began to turn fast as I had the fleeting thought of bashing my evil friend over the head with a frying pan, but it was too late, other guests were arriving. I had to greet them. I couldn't tell if Ted was afraid or entranced by the she-devil.

Luckily, Matilda grabbed him by the hand, ushering him back to their game.

I had a very bad feeling about things.

Chapter Eight

"Stop playing God with other people's lives," Javier scolded.

One thing about Javier, he always stays on message. He'd followed me into the kitchen when I'd gone to refill the bowl of mashed potatoes.

"Let me tell you something, Javier: Ted is *not* going home with Lisa. She'll eat him alive. How can you think that's okay? You *know* how she is."

He shook his head, muttering in Spanish under his breath, "*Mi esposa es muy loco*," which, loosely translated, means I'm nuts.

"I resent that remark," I protested.

Dinner, surprisingly, had been going fairly well. Chris gave a lovely grace, thanking God for all of the abundance and things for which we were all grateful, after which Frank said, ever-so eloquently, "Rub a dub dub, bring on the grub," and smiled, proud of himself.

"Classy, Pop. Real classy," Javier said.

"Thanks, *mijo*."

My parents think everything is funny and laughed at Lisa's witty banter, and drank. They'd recently returned from a trip to Taos, New Mexico, and my mother was explaining in great detail about the different rocks she'd purchased and their respective healing properties while my brother looked askance at their New Age talk.

"This agate is particularly good for promoting creativity and self-expression," she was explaining to my wide-eyed sister-in-law Hilda, who seemed to be absorbing the crazy talk. I couldn't help myself.

"Mom, you don't really believe that bullshit, do you?"

I probably shouldn't have said that. Silence overtook the table—uncomfortable silence—for a few seconds. You could hear the crickets chirping; I could feel my husband's disapproval. Javier was shaking his head at me; Chris shot a hand over his mouth, stifling a laugh. Dad sat nodding in agreement with me as Mom laughed it off.

"I *do* believe it. I really do."

"Sally," Lisa purred, "when you were in Taos, did they have any rocks for getting it on? You know, like sex rocks?"

The crickets returned again. I made a quick note to self: next time, sit next to Lisa so I can kick her under the table when I need to.

Ted was ashen. Chris let out an embarrassed giggle. Mom waved Lisa off with a laugh. "They do. You'd want rose quartz, the love stone."

Lisa was taking notes, typing "rose quartz" on her iPhone.

Conversation resumed, drinking resumed. All was well again. Except, as fate would have it, Lisa ended up sitting directly across from Ted. My worst fear.

I sat in turmoil as I watched the whole ghastly scene play out before my eyes. She'd stare at him as if she wanted to undress him. With her teeth. I tried in vain to stretch my leg out far enough under the table so I could kick her but ended up kicking Rudy, Javier's younger brother, instead.

"Sorry," I apologized with a weak smile.

When Lisa wasn't undressing poor Ted with her eyes and had turned her attention to visiting with Javier's sister-in-law Hilda who was seated to her right, I watched as Ted looked at her with his lonely eyes. It was almost too much to bear. And *not* what I had planned. I had to do something to get them apart.

But what if Javier was right? What if I *was* playing God with other peoples' lives? The thought was a serious bummer; I sat there and contemplated my wretchedness.

Fortunately, since contemplating my own wretchedness is one of my least favorite things to do, I decided to instead bask in the glow of family; to simply be thankful for the fact that we were all healthy, slightly crazy and off-kilter, but at least we didn't want to kill each other. There was no full-blown animosity or wishing one of the group was somewhere else, with the possible exception of Frank and his obvious discomfiture being within close range of Lisa, but that was a mystery for another time.

I listened to my parents tell their wacky stories about following their vision quests, and the noteworthy sweat lodge experience last summer involving one of the guests, too much peyote, and streaking. The children chattered and played with their food. Chris told priest jokes which, maybe not surprisingly, aren't all that funny. Frank continued to avoid eye contact with Lisa. Javier laughed as Ted looked awkward, but only half as awkward as he did when he'd arrived. There were so many things to be thankful for. And somewhere around mile marker one hour and fifteen minutes into our meal, it hit me: I needed to get Ted much drunker.

It was time to switch from wine to gin.

Unfortunately, as I excused myself to make my shy friend a cocktail, Lisa followed me into the kitchen, claws out and ready. She leaned against the countertop, eyeing me with curiosity.

"So what's the story with Ted? Why haven't you introduced us before this?" she demanded. "He's shy, isn't he?"

"Now, where is that gin?" I opened the upper liquor cabinet doors, looking for the bottle. "I thought we had a new bottle. Ted loves the gin. He's a big fan," I said, then mimicked someone drinking, tipping my head back and making a little *glug glug* sound.

"Fun," Lisa said, animated now. "When you find it, make mine a double."

Great.

"So how's business?" I asked, making conversation, hoping to change the subject while I sliced a lime into wedges and got the bag of ice out of the freezer. Gin and tonics are a specialty of mine. A pitcher of G&Ts is like mother's milk—a gift from the gods. And a good G&T is deceptively strong. Ted would be crawling around like a little baby by the end of the night. Lisa would have to close up shop and go home, talons empty. I was doing this for his own good. Someone had to save him from the she-devil's clutches.

"Oh, it's picked up a little lately. Got a new client a couple of weeks ago." She became serious, and said in a low whisper, "He likes to wear diapers."

"You don't say," I said in a deadpan voice. I've heard a lot of interesting things about Lisa's line of work, so much so that I tend not to get surprised anymore. "That sounds a little awkward. Do you have to change him?"

"Well, I suppose I could. But I'd charge *way* more for that, so it hasn't come up yet."

Lisa is a bona fide dominatrix. In all seriousness. She makes her money by bossing and whipping men—on occasion women —into shape. It's like a dream come true for her. I mean, she *really is* living her dream. When Oprah encouraged the American woman to follow her passion, it was like she was talking directly to Lisa.

Ever since we were in kindergarten, she's been a dominatrix. The boys on the playground feared her; the girls followed her. I guess you could say it's her unique gift.

It's not at all difficult to understand why men fall all over themselves just to be spanked by her. With her long thick red hair and green eyes, she's a real-life Cat Woman. Actually, now that I think about it, she *has* that costume in her rotation, complete with the thigh-high black leather boots.

Lisa is the type of person who walks into a room and commands attention. The thought of her taking poor innocent Ted and turning him into a diaper-wearing infant was too much to bear, so I made her drink a triple.

"Here, try this," I said, handing her the highball glass. "Tell me what you think."

"Mmmm. It's good, but could you put some gin in there?"

She's funny. I tilted the bottle and began to pour.

"Much better." She gave me an evil wink. "Can I take Ted's out to him?" she asked with a purr.

"Sure. Thanks so much," I said with a disingenuous smile. It was almost too easy.

As the gin flowed like water, and the empty wine bottle count continued to mount, our guests were gradually peeled away from us. First Rudy, Hilda and the kids, since they knew better than to stick around. My brother Chris left before things got ugly, which is always a wise thing for a man of God to do. My parents followed, also wanting to escape the fray. I, surprisingly, remained clearheaded, feeling it was best to keep my wits about me as the others lost theirs.

Once Matilda was put to bed, the serious drinking started, with the remaining group sitting around the coffee table playing quarters. That's right. Quarters. It was as if I'd taken a trip back to high school.

First Javier gave Ted a brief tutorial, coaching him on how to bounce the quarter off the table just right to get it to land in the glass of beer.

"That seems impossible," he complained.

"No, no. Here, like this."

Javier bounced the quarter like a pro. It landed in the cup with a splash. Naturally, he handed the cup to Ted.

"Bottoms, up, Ted."

Ted was toast.

At ten-thirty, I pulled my father-in-law away from the quarters game and asked him nicely, "Frank, would you mind giving Lisa a ride home?" She was now three sheets to the wind and unable to drive. It was a small victory for the good guys.

"Oh, no. No, no, no, no," he said, waving his hands and shaking his head with force.

I cocked my head to the side, confused by his extreme reaction. I was intrigued. His anti-Lisa stance had been going on for quite some time, and I'd never had the nerve to ask him for an explanation. My curiosity had finally gotten the best of me. I had to ask.

"Frank, you've *got* to tell me. I'm dying here. Exactly *what* happened between you two?"

His jaw tightened; he was tense now. He sighed. "All right. I'll make you a deal," he whispered. "I tell you what happened, and you don't ever mention it again."

"Deal."

"Wait. That's not it. This is a two-part deal. The second part is: don't ever mention this to Javier."

"Got it."

"Do you promise?" he asked with his brown eyes fixed and narrowed on mine in a steely gaze.

"Cross my heart and hope to die," I said, crossing my heart.

"You better sit down for this," he said. "Let's go into the kitchen."

We snuck off, extra careful to be out of earshot, and sat down at my kitchen table.

"Do you need something strong?" I asked.

"No, no." He waved my offer away. "I'm just going to come right out and say it."

I stared at him; he stared at me. The silence was a little uncomfortable. I started humming the *Jeopardy* thinking music; he gave me an exasperated look, coughed once, took a deep breath, summoning his inner resources.

"I spent a weekend with Lisa. Most of the time I was handcuffed to her bed."

I didn't mean to scream; it was totally involuntary, but I did. Scream. It was a short scream because Frank immediately clasped his hand over my mouth, apologizing as he did so. His hand was a little clammy, too, which made it that much worse.

"Sorry, *mija*. I had to do that," he whispered. "Can I take my hand away now?"

"Mmm-hmmm," I mumbled through his hand, nodding. He took his hand away and then pulled his bandanna from the top of his head down, covering his face in shame, but really more as a joke, laughing as he did so.

"Frank," I laughed, "you pervy old dog!" I teased, absorbing the shock.

"I knew it was a mistake telling you," he said with regret, shifting in his seat uncomfortably.

Actually, the more I thought about it, the more embarrassed I became. Wasn't I the one who'd brought a dominatrix into my father-in-law's life? What did that say about me? Isn't the saying, "A man is known by the company he keeps"? In this case "woman"?

"Well, at least things won't be awkward between us now," I said with a laugh. Then I couldn't help myself, I had to rub it in a little. "So, Frank, when you're not *too* tied up, would you mind giving Lisa a ride home?"

"Do it yourself, *mija*. I'm not that hard up. To be honest, I don't want to be alone with her. And *don't* tell Javier," he said, pointing his finger at me. "You *promised* me now." He said the last part with added force.

For as long as I live, I may never get the picture of naked Frank cuffed to Lisa's headboard out of my head. That genie had been let out of the bottle. And now I'd have to summon every bit of strength I had, I mean, it would take *everything* in my power not to tell Javier this red-hot piece of information. Poor Frank.

Sometimes knowing too much can be a real curse. And I definitely knew more than I ever wanted to.

Chapter Nine

I drove a drunken, but surprisingly agreeable, Lisa home shortly after midnight, with Javier following behind in her Smart Car. Her Echo Park apartment—the same one we'd shared years before when we were young and carefree and broke—was close by. She mumbled and drooled in my car, singing "We Are the Champions" at the top of her lungs, rocking back and forth, crashing into me every few seconds. I didn't bother shushing her, which is unfortunate, because she's a terribly bad singer.

I parked, and Javier helped me in the frustrating process of extracting her from my car, coaxing and urging her out before beginning the equally impossible task of getting her into the elevator as she stumbled along.

"Where's my drink?" she asked, quite drunkenly, slurring her words.

She had dragon's breath.

We lurched along, coaxing her down the empty corridor of her apartment building; her arm was draped around Javier's shoulder as he half carried her down the hall to her unit.

"What about the neighbors?" Javier whispered to me.

"Don't worry. It's not a problem."

And it wasn't. The woman who lived to the right of Lisa was deaf. The guy who lived to the left of Lisa was, literally, a circus freak. Jax was a human bulletin board. And I really wish that weren't true, but it is. He worked in a sideshow where he'd let people staple money to his body. The higher the bill's denomination, the dicier it got. For a twenty-dollar bill, he'd let a person staple the twenty directly onto his forehead. I'd never actually witnessed this, thank God. I don't know what he'd allow for one hundred dollars; I didn't even want to go there in my mind, but in comparison, he made Lisa look like a demure suburban housewife.

While I fumbled with her keys, searching for the right one, she broke away from Javier, tottered a few steps in her heels, and fell, slamming into Jax's front door with a loud *thud*. Fifteen seconds later, the door opened and a tattooed head poked out.

"Hey," Jax said with a little nod.

"Hi, Jax," I said.

He took in the scene. I volunteered, "She's had a little too much to drink. Everything's under control."

"Do you need help putting her to bed?" He seemed a little too eager to volunteer for tucking-in duty, creeping me out a little.

"No, that won't be necessary," I said, all light and airy to keep things between us on a friendly level.

"Cool. 'Night." He popped his head back inside his apartment and closed the door. Javier and I exchanged glances. He sighed, saying simply, "Why me?"

I nodded in agreement. Jav was right. I'm fairly sure the Pilgrims never envisioned drunken strumpets and human pincushions when they created their holiday.

Thanksgiving evening was *never* meant to be like this.

Lisa's apartment, on first glance by the casual observer, seems normal enough. It's only when one starts to look around that they notice something is a little out of the ordinary. For instance, the intricately carved wooden bowl sitting on the sofa's side table is a lovely decoration, but it's also filled with packages of condoms, multicolored, various sizes, some textured for added sensation, some not.

The bookcase next to the entertainment center has a shelf with little bottles of body lotions and oils lined up neatly as if they're hair products on display at a salon. Then there's the room devoted to nothing but leather—whips, bridles, dog leashes, studded collars—you name it, it's in there. Some people take their work home with them; Lisa's home is her very own sex lab/playground.

Javier was trying to reason with her as he walked her through her living room. "Come on now, walk one foot in front of the other," he said in a vain attempt to keep her upright, but she was like a ragdoll, falling out from under him in every direction.

"Let's get her into bed," I said, taking her other arm and looping it around my shoulder as we walked her down the short hallway, past prosaic family photos intermixed with artistic nudes.

"Where's my drink," she demanded again.

"Shut up, drunkie," I barked. Javier shot me a surprised look. I have to admit, it felt good to be bossing *her* around for a change.

I paused outside her bedroom door, with her head propped against my shoulder, and looked at my husband who struggled to keep his half of Lisa upright.

"Javier, I have to warn you about her bedroom. It may not be what you'd expect."

He gave me a patronizing look. "I think I can handle it, babe."

"Well, don't say I didn't warn you."

I pushed the door open with my foot, and we entered Lisa's Shangri-La.

"There you go," I said to our drunk girl as we gently deposited her onto her bed. She immediately rolled over onto her stomach, let out an enormous belch, and splayed her arms and legs in all directions, taking up most of the mattress's space. I slipped her shoes off as Javier took in the room, making a slow three hundred-sixty-degree turn. His eyes were wide, like a child who's seeing Santa's workshop for the very first time, taking in the wonder.

There was no escaping the black leather swing suspended from an eyebolt in the ceiling. It was *the* elephant in the room. My childlike husband was drawn to it as if it were a magnet and he was Ironman. He stood there beholding its magic.

"Babe, do you think we could try—"

"Absolutely not," I snapped. "Who knows what's gone on, on top of that—that *thing*." I shuddered. "Let's get out of here. She's fine."

Javier walked around it but didn't touch it, clearly mesmerized by its power.

I gave Lisa's arm a little nudge as she lay sprawled out; she snorted.

"Do you think she'll be okay?" Javier asked, his eyebrows knitted in worry.

I'd seen her like this many times before—we'd lived together during our joint halfhearted attempt at college, plus a few years after—but it touched me, how concerned he was about my now loudly snoring friend. Javier had such a caring way about him.

In the most improbable of circumstances, standing in my drunken friend's sex cave, I found myself having a moment. Life can be so crappy sometimes. We slog through the muck day after day. People we love get sick; they die. We grieve, we fight, we struggle sometimes just to get through the day. We spend nights lying in bed looking up at the ceiling, questioning our very existence, which, luckily, doesn't happen too often for me. Still, I felt extra grateful for Javier—for sleeping next to me at night, for talking me down from the ledge during those rare moments when my soul is filled with self-doubt and angst, sure that I'm worth absolutely nothing to anybody anywhere.

In that moment, I felt grateful for everything, but perhaps most of all, I felt gratitude that he'd saved me from a life of searching, disappointment, and loneliness. I'm an acquired taste, I know this, not a person easy to live with, let alone put up with for any appreciable amount of time.

I watched him as he worried about Ms. Thing passed out on her bed, and I gave his neck a little nuzzle.

"Don't ever leave me," I said to him.

"I won't, babe. As long as you get us one of these."

He was pointing to the swing. I smacked him on the shoulder. We left Lisa; her snores reverberated, echoing off the walls, to go back home and check on our other drunk friend.

Chapter Ten

Ted awoke with a start, most likely because I was sitting at the foot of the bed in the spare room watching his chest rise and fall, waiting for him to stir. Dave had burst into the room in his customary loutish way and was nudging him, placing his snout squarely on top of Ted's chest. Dave was nothing if not a caring dog, and evidently he thought Ted might possibly be dead.

The quarters game had taken a turn for the worse, and Ted started to go severely south by eleven p.m. Frank and Javier helped put him to bed somewhere around eleven-thirty, shortly before we drove drunken Lisa home. When I saw him last, the menfolk were carrying him to the bathroom so he could throw up.

Dave licked the side of Ted's battered face. First one eye opened, then the other. He tried to focus.

"I'm sorry. I didn't mean to startle you," I apologized.

He sat up quickly, still wearing his dress shirt, which was now rumpled, and slacks from the night before. He rubbed his temple and ran a hand through his thick dirty blond hair, which was a mess.

"What time is it? And why do I feel like I've been run over by a truck?"

"It's twelve-thirty, and you were really shitfaced, dear. Forgive my language."

He shook his head, then held it in his hands. "Ugh. I'm so dizzy."

I said no more and handed him the still-fizzing glass of Alka-Seltzer I'd been holding. He drank it quickly.

"Would you mind? I've got to use the bathroom," he said, working his way off the bed slowly. He resembled an old man with creaky bones. I nodded. "But could you wait here a minute? There's something I wanted to ask you," he said.

"I'll be here."

Sunlight streamed through the crack in the blinds. Ted was in misery. My evil plan had been successful, but my victory seemed hollow. I think that may be due to something we humans beings like to call a conscience.

I was still sitting on the bed when he returned.

"I'm a little embarrassed. I don't usually wake up like this, hungover at someone's house."

He stood in the middle of the room, his shoulders slumped, a shell of his former self.

"Hold on a minute. Have a seat," I instructed my patient. "I'll be right back."

I went out to the kitchen and returned with a hand towel that I'd wet with warm water to use as a compress. Maternal feelings were coming to the surface in big emotional waves. I felt an incredible urge to help him, to put him on my lap and stroke his hair. Poor baby.

I sat down on the bed next to him, but not so close as to invade his personal space.

"Here, put this on your forehead."

He took the warm compress and pressed it to his face and neck.

"Mmm. That feels nice."

My guilt was beginning to overwhelm me. He looked like such a vulnerable little boy sitting there. Innocent. I wanted to feed him little bites of soup and fluff his pillow. The need to apologize enveloped me; I could contain it no longer.

"I'm so sorry. This is all my fault. I never should have subjected you to all of us. We're *way* too much to take, especially all at once. And I should *never* have let you play a game of quarters with those jackals."

Ted let out a little groan, holding the warm towel up to his face, dabbing his forehead.

"You know something, Julia?"

"What?"

"I had a really good time."

He had a weak smile on his face now. I wanted to kiss his little cheek and pat it, but I stopped myself. It was a sweet thing for him to say, as if the night of drunken debauching had changed our relationship from one of distant colleagues to friends, and I didn't want to let him down. My resolve to help him, instead of weakening, grew stronger.

"Well, that's so nice to hear," I said with a smile. "That helps a little. Now I don't feel so guilty about abusing you."

Ted gave another weak smile.

"Wait here. Let me see how Javier's coming with the menudo. It's known for its healing powers. One bowl, and you'll be as good as new." I moved to get up and leave him, but he stopped me, surprising me by softly, tentatively, touching my arm.

"Wait, Julia. Can I ask you something?"

"Of course."

I sat back down on the bed next to him and waited for him to gather his thoughts. I watched him as he looked down at the wet towel in his hands, then down at his feet.

"Was there something you wanted to talk about?" I offered, gently pressing him.

"I was wondering about Lisa."

Ah. There it was. It figured. She'd evidently made an impact on him. But of course she did; it was silly of me to think otherwise.

"What did you need to know?" I said sweetly, innocently.

"Well, what can you tell me about her? What does she do, for instance?"

His eyes were wide now, like a puppy's. Hopeful.

He'd asked the million-dollar question. But how could I crush him by telling him the truth? The poor guy. I hesitated as different answers caromed around inside my head, bouncing off each other.

What if Lisa was "the one" though? It was an improbable thought. Lisa worked her way through men the same way a little kid starts at one end of a bag of Halloween candy and works his way down to the bottom, throwing out lesser pieces such as open-bin caramels and butterscotches like old news. The image of Lisa devouring him and tossing his remains aside, heartbroken and adrift, was too much. I had to tell him the truth, as kindly as possible.

"She's a sex worker, Ted."

He winced as if I'd hit him over the head with a blunt object.

"Headache?" I asked.

"Yeah," he mumbled. "Erm, did you say 'sex worker'?"

"Yes, of sorts."

The puzzled look on his face compelled me to explain further.

Someday, when Matilda is older, I'll have to have serious talks with her about getting her period, life in general, sex, men's and women's issues, even politics. This was sort of like my training. Ted's inexperience in the ways of the world was pretty evident. I took a deep breath and trudged ahead.

"Ted, let me ask you something: are you familiar with the whole idea of bondage? You know, S&M?"

His eyes were like two soccer balls, very wide. I continued.

"Lisa is what you'd call a dominatrix. Men visit her who like to be bossed around a bit and spanked."

"With whips?" he said, trying to grasp the whole scenario, his eyes even wider now.

"Yes, whips."

"Bullwhips?"

"Um, perhaps. Or maybe even an open palm. I'm in no way an expert though," I added quickly, feeling like I needed to add that little caveat. He was silent, quietly processing this new information—I could almost see the central processing chip in his brain glowing bright blue—as I got up to leave him, feeling a tad wretched. "When you feel like it, come out and join us, have some soup."

He gave a little nod, then winced again, rubbing his temples.

Poor guy. The deed was done. Any illusions he'd had about my friend were now dashed. And I didn't have to lie or misrepresent things. The truth was the truth. Ted was much too shy and conservative for someone like Lisa. They were most definitely *not* a match, in my humble amateur matchmaker's opinion.

The aroma of garlic, onions, and chili peppers filled the kitchen as I went to check on Javier's progress with his special menudo. He stood next to his pot of soup, stirring in a bit of cayenne pepper and fussing over it. I experienced another twinge of guilt. *What if Ted and Lisa were meant to be together?* It was a beyond-ridiculous thought. I laughed at myself, feeling silly even thinking it.

Sometimes my imagination gets away from me. Sometimes.

We heard Frank's deep hello as he opened the front door after first giving a little knock.

"Hello? Anybody home?"

"Come in, Pop," Javier yelled out to him from the kitchen. He was taking the tall stockpot from the burner to set it onto the ceramic trivet on the kitchen table.

Frank was dressed in his usual crisply pressed jeans and immaculate white T-shirt. If he were to ever show up wearing anything else, I'm sure I'd fall over on the spot and die. After a night of heavy drinking, he appeared no worse for the wear.

He came over to where I was, standing next to the silverware drawer, and gave me a kiss on the cheek as I took spoons out of the open drawer.

"*Hola*, beautiful."

"*Hola*, darling. It's so good to see you. Have a seat. You're just in time for lunch."

He took a seat near the wall, pushing his sunglasses up to the top of his head. "I came to check on our patient. How is he?" he said with a low voice, not wanting to disturb our depleted friend.

Javier handed his father a steaming bowl, shaking his head, making a little clucking sound. "I'm afraid we killed him."

Frank's eyes got wide.

"Ted's a little under the weather," I said.

"Poor guy," he said, and burst into a deep roaring laugh before plunging a spoon into his soup.

Funny, he didn't seem to be all *that* sorry for him.

"Well, we all pay our dues," he said philosophically. "It was *time* for his first hangover, *mija*," he said in response to the look of disapproval on my face, hitting the tabletop with his hand, as if a hangover were an absolute necessary rite of passage.

We each have our views about life; Frank's were simple, annoying, truths.

Dave the dog joined us, followed by Matilda, who was wearing a pink ballet leotard and sparkly tutu. Ted eventually hobbled out, squeezing into the chair next to Frank, clutching his aching head with one hand. The small dinette was about to burst at the seams, but Dave tucked his shaggy, eighty-pound frame under the table, invisible to all.

"This is good," Ted said. He'd somehow managed to gather his resources and balance a spoonful of soup and bring it up to his lips, sipping gently. "What's in it, anyway?"

I exchanged glances with Javier and Frank. We were quiet. Poor gringo Ted had never been exposed to the mystical healing powers of menudo.

"It's better not knowing," I said finally, when the silence went on too long.

"Like sausage, it's best not to know what goes in there," Javier said wisely.

Frank roared with laughter this time, slamming his hand down on the table, causing the loose stockpot lid to tremble a bit. The whole thing was a big joke to him. I wanted to kick him under the table, but Dave was in the way.

"It's tripe," Matilda chimed in, happily munching the soup made from the intestines of something or other. Cow, I think.

Ted's face turned a light shade of green as Frank slapped him on the back.

"Breakfast of champions, *mijo*."

"Or lunch," I volunteered with a half-smile.

"Same difference." Frank shrugged and turned to Ted. "You're one of the family now."

I wasn't sure by Ted's expression if that was a *good* thing or not.

Chapter Eleven

Lisa's voice on the other end of the phone was low, barely rising above a whisper.

"I can't get out of bed. I'm dying, but I'm starving. Bring me food."

"Why don't you call Jax," I suggested. Her sideshow neighbor had an obvious crush. I mean, it would be obvious to the most casual observer, the way he seemed to hang on her every word, grateful for any crumb of attention she happened to throw his way. He'd be over to her place in a shot, feeding her by hand, probably doing her laundry as well as any other chores she had for him. All she needed to do was whistle.

They'd never gotten together, even for one night. This fact alone was extraordinary, knowing my friend and her habits. Jax viewed Lisa as some sort of neoprene dream girl. I'd often wondered why nothing had happened between them, but Lisa assured me this was most definitely *not* a good idea, showing surprising maturity on her part. It struck me as kind of a cosmic joke that a masochistic human bulletin board had unwittingly moved next door to someone who inflicted pain for a living. It was almost *too* convenient and probably why they'd never work as a couple.

"Oh, I don't want to do that. He'd get wrong ideas. He'd be all hopeful, and I'm not the type to raise false hope." *That* was an understatement. "What did you put in my drink anyway," she said, her tone accusatory.

I ignored her; she'd asked for it. Correction. Demanded it.

"How about if I send Frank over with some menudo," I asked innocently just to see what she'd say to the suggestion of my father-in-law showing up at her apartment. My devil horns were starting to come out.

"Oh, um, that's all right. Forget it."

Hmm. That's what I thought.

"All right. I'll be over in an hour."

I had to send Ted home first.

After showering and dressing in spare clothes supplied by Javier, three Tylenols, and two cups of coffee later, our friend was feeling more of himself than when he'd first awakened. I'd played with the thought of arranging a quick introduction between him and Sylvia before he went home—all I'd need do was make a quick phone call—but discarded the idea. I wanted them to see each other at their very best, not with him pale and hung over.

Besides, if this was going to be the match that worked, things would have to be perfect. It was too soon.

I walked him out to his car, parked in front of the house, and we said our goodbyes. He accepted my hug, actually hugging me back. Our bodies made light contact, and it wasn't one of those awkward hugs with space in between. This one was real.

"Will you come back and have dinner with us again?" I asked as he got into his hybrid-electric car.

"I will. I just need to get healthy again."

We shared a laugh as Frank and Javier waved from the porch.

"Come back next week, I'll bring tequila," Frank called out to him, laughing like a big idiot, waving enthusiastically to his new playmate. I wanted to smack my father-in-law for many reasons, the biggest one involving the image of him handcuffed to Lisa's bed. It remained burned into my brain.

My life is a little *too* interesting sometimes.

After explaining to Matilda why it was best that she stay home— that "Aunt Lisa is a little ill"—and assuring her I wouldn't catch her sickness, I packed soup for my invalid. On the short drive over, I reflected on our friendship. Javier had never really understood why, as he put it, I put up with her. But our relationship was deeper than he gave it credit for. There were the nights when she'd lovingly held my hair back as I puked into a trash can in some club's parking lot, or the times she'd defended me from unwanted advances on account of her being such a scary bad-ass.

Our time together in college was the stuff legends are made of. Our parents collectively still hadn't forgiven us for the semester in London where we both ended up owing the college credits and all of that money wasted on books that were never once cracked open. Still feeling guilty about that one.

Our plan had been simple: we enrolled at Orange Coast Community College fresh out of high school. The first year, we both worked hard; I earned a perfect 4.0. Of course, my classes were Drama, PE, and Poli-Sci, but still, I *earned* those grades. Lisa did the same, slogging through her English, math, and welding classes.

Our parents were so proud of us when our invitations to participate in the European studies program arrived in the mail. The whole thing was too easy. And it was like giving a giant bag of lollipops to a couple of greedy four-year-olds. I majored in pub crawls; Lisa majored in men. But I did see a few extremely high-ceilinged cathedrals, and Lisa got to take a tour of the Tower of London and its assortment of medieval torture devices, taking notes as she did so; so it wasn't a total loss.

Years later, when Lisa followed her life's real passion by becoming a certified dominatrix—she took actual live classes with a real instructor—I felt happy for her. I really did. I mean, there are all *kinds* of people in this world. Who's to say something is perverted or wrong as long as it's between two, even three, consenting adults? And Lisa has explained to me that there's a whole under-served segment of society who would live half-lives of shame and self-loathing if it weren't for her selfless, helpful actions. So I guess, in a sense, Lisa was a leather-bound hero goddess. I don't see her winning any awards any time soon. Maybe she should.

I let myself in to my old apartment, not bothering to knock first. Somehow Lisa had been able to hobble to the front door and unlock it for me before hobbling back to bed, probably while on a quest for something to drink.

It had been years since the two of us had moved in together after our short college experiment. A rent-controlled dwelling of any kind in Los Angeles is not something to take lightly. The three-story building remained largely the same but was in serious need of a new coat of exterior paint where it was chipped and peeling in places.

My patient was bundled under a heap of blankets moaning quietly. When she saw me, she moaned loudly for my benefit.

"I'm going to die. I've decided. I might as well pack it in now," she whimpered. Pathetic.

"I've brought some soup. Javier made it with his own hands," I said cheerfully.

"Feed me," she begged with sorrowful puppy eyes.

I pulled the one lone folding chair that was sitting next to the "swing," over to the bed. I felt a little weird, like I wanted to drape a sheet over the big black leather thing so it wouldn't be so damned distracting. Some things are hard to ignore, especially when one conjures up images of leather-bound men with scary Lisa sitting on top of it doing questionable things to them. I shuddered at the thought.

She sat up, propping herself against the pillows, and frowned, the movement apparently too strenuous.

"Here you go," I said, holding a spoon to her lips.

"Mmm." She tasted it. The Dragon's eyes grew wide with approval. "Give me that," she commanded, grabbing the Tupperware container and spoon out of my hands.

She dug in, making loud slurping sounds. "God, this is so good. I want Javier to be my personal chef."

"Okay, *that's* not going to happen."

She made a face and kept eating.

"Since you seem to be feeling better, I'll be on my way," I said, seizing the opportunity to extricate myself from her sickroom.

"Wait." She reached out, touching my arm. "How's Ted? What's he doing today?" she said in a small voice.

Ugh. Not you too.

How in the world were two people so ill-suited in likes, dislikes, and personality traits so attracted to each other? Of all improbable scenarios, this would have been the least likely. I was feeling thoroughly discombobulated.

"I'm not gonna lie; he wasn't feeling great. Why the sudden interest anyway?" I asked with narrowed eyes.

"Here. Would you take this?"

She handed the half-empty container of soup back to me, took a breath, and slumped against the pillows as if the action had taken every bit of strength she was able to muster.

"You know something? I'm sick of being alone. I think I'm ready to enter into a long-term type of arrangement."

She was completely serious.

"As in you and one person only? The whole monogamy thing?" I asked, a tad skeptically.

"Yeah, I *think* so."

The part about monogamy seemed to have thrown her a little bit.

"I don't know, Lisa. Ted's a nice guy, but…he's so different. And his family's pretty conservative. Mormon I think."

"Oh, fuck."

"Well, they're nice people…"

"They're also totally patriarchal. I mean, what is all that bullshit about one husband and multiple wives? Why not one wife with multiple husbands?"

And…she was off, having her own fantasy now where she was the leader of her own male commune.

"Why don't you start your own religion? You could have your own sex cult. A matriarchy of sorts."

This option was being mulled over; I could tell because she had the look of someone in deep thought, like both hamsters were running in circles around the wheel in her head. In the *same* direction. She sighed. "Maybe not. But I do like the idea of being the queen."

"I know you do, sweetie."

The combination of Lisa and Ted would never work, of this I was almost one hundred percent sure. And I'm usually not wrong about these things. Okay, I am. But I had an *extra*-strong feeling about this one.

In a final act of charity, I filled a pitcher with water, a squirt of lemon, and some ice, and placed it by her bedside table along with a bottle of Extra Strength Tylenol, warning her: "Remember, only two at a time." She promptly swallowed three tablets.

"I said two."

"Three *is* my two."

I snatched the bottle away and went home, vowing that the next year's day after Thanksgiving would not involve my playing nursemaid to hung over friends. I'd go shopping instead.

Chapter Twelve

Religion has always been something I've been a little sketchy on. Organized religion, to be more precise. It could have something to do with the fact that my parents, who were—and still are—spiritual people, were religious experimenters. Seekers, if you will. My dad to this day teaches a comparative religion course through the Education Annex, "Religion: From Gnosticism to Fundamentalism." I've taken it, and it's a *lot* more fun than it sounds.

While I was growing up, they had their Buddhist phase, the Hindu experience, Self-Realization Fellowship, and Transcendental Meditation (TM), to name a few. This *may* have something to do with my feeling of not quite belonging to any one organized group. It may also explain how my brother became an Episcopal priest. One shared experience, two vastly different outcomes.

Still, with my lack of formal religious training, even *I* know that falling in love with someone who's taken an oath of poverty and celibacy is probably not a person's best idea, so when Sylvia insisted that I accompany her to Mass to check out dreamy Father Tom, I knew it was a bad idea. Furthermore, because of our young friendship, I couldn't tell her of my own reconnaissance mission some weeks previous. I had a feeling she may not *understand*.

I tried reasoning with her one last time as we drove the few short blocks to St. Mary's.

"Um, Sylvia, do you think it's a good idea to stalk your priest?"

She waved me off as a worrier. "Oh, it's not stalking. It's not like that at all. I mean, he's my priest. I can see him privately any time I need to."

Yeah, like *that* was a good idea.

"So what do you expect to get out of this 'relationship' anyway?" I asked, air quoting the word "relationship," which seemed to set her off a little.

"Julia! Why can't you be more supportive of me? You're always talking about how I should meet someone. Well, here someone is. Can't you go along with this? Just this once?"

I nodded slowly, remaining quiet, humoring her, as she pulled her car into the church's parking lot. It was a few minutes after nine, and it was freezing for Los Angeles. Winter had decided to make its presence known. I pulled my coat closer, buttoning the top button.

"I hope the heat works," I grumbled; Sylvia ignored me. Her midcalf-length trench, scarf and hat pulled down over her forehead made her almost unrecognizable, which probably wasn't a *bad* thing since we were there with ulterior motives.

Once again, I had to explain to Javier why I was going to morning Mass when it wasn't a major holiday. Christmas was still three weeks away. If we were *very* good, we'd attend midnight Mass and be set until Easter.

"Where are you going? I'm making waffles with Tillie," he said as he walked into the bedroom wearing his Kiss the Cook apron.

I sat on my side of the bed and pulled my boots over my jeans. The thought of waffles was tempting, but I shook it off. I had to stay strong. "I'm going with Sylvia."

By the way his eyebrows were raised, I could tell he was curious.

"I'll be back in an hour. Save me one?" I folded my hands in supplication, giving him my biggest puppy eyes. He's never been able to refuse "the eyes."

"All right," he said, a bit grudgingly, "we'll wait."

He mumbled something under his breath as he left the room. I could have sworn I heard the words "crazy wife" in there somewhere, an all-too common refrain that I resented. He had no idea what I was involved in; it was mean of him to naturally assume I was up to something. Of course, he was right, but still.

Sylvia walked up the center aisle first, picking a pew in the back, paused, genuflected, and crossed herself. I mimicked her actions self-consciously. When I cross myself, I always feel like I'm doing it wrong. I'm never really sure whether to cross from the left shoulder and draw my hand over to the right, or start with the right, moving over to the left, so I intermix and do the whole thing quickly so no one notices my errors.

Before sitting down, she knelt down on the kneeler to pray, so I did the same. We had the pew to ourselves; I jabbed her arm with my elbow.

"You know, you can't pray for *that*."

"What do you mean?" she whispered indignantly. "How do you know what I'm praying for anyway? You're not supposed to be *judging* my prayers."

"Oh, I *know*," I said, giving her a judgmental look.

It's one thing to pray for God to send you a mate; it's another to ask God to be your partner in crime. What Sylvia was asking seemed to be overstepping. But, then again, who was I to be the arbiter of all things prayer-related?

I clasped my hands and closed my eyes, but I couldn't help but glance over at Sylvia. The look on her face was one of serenity, as if she'd been transported to another place. There was almost a glow about her. I wondered if my face ever got a glow when I prayed. Probably not. But I prayed. For Javier and Matilda —our little family. I prayed for my parents. I prayed for my brother Chris, for Frank, Ted, Sylvia, Lisa, and all the other lonely people I knew. It was short and sweet; no special favors were asked.

Praying is not a specialty of mine, but it's something I've talked to my parents about, and I've had many conversations on the topic with Chris, the expert. One conversation with my priestly brother on the subject was particularly memorable: he emphasized how God is not a slot machine; he's not going to send you the winning lotto numbers and that kind of thing. So I've kept that in mind over the years and tried to rein myself in.

We sat back up on the hard, cold pew and waited for the service to begin. The stained glass window closest to me depicted a very large angel, clad in a billowy white robe. The angel had the most mournful eyes—eyes that seemed to know something. I found it somewhat uncomfortable, although not necessarily creepy. Lost in thought, I wondered what dark secrets the angel knew about mankind.

Sylvia nudged me in the side, hard, breaking my trance.

"What?"

"He's coming," she whispered, breathless and atwitter.

"Settle down now," I said, reaching over and patting her shoulder.

Her breathing was beginning to sound labored. I looked over at my friend who appeared to be on the verge of hyperventilation. "Okay. I've seen him," I whispered. "Maybe we should go," I suggested. Javier's waffles were calling me home. His waffles always come out crispy on the edges and fluffy in the middle. I don't know how he does it, but he uses his Grandma Terry's own recipe. They're totally worth cutting church early for. And, truth be told, Sylvia was starting to freak me out; she seemed a bit too overwrought by the sight of the man who, I was now convinced, was her obsession.

The look on her face told me my suggestion would go unheeded.

"We're not going *now*. How can you suggest that? We're here. I'm not leaving," she announced with a wild look in her eyes.

"All right, all right. We'll stay. But you need to calm down."

A man two pews up from us kept turning his head to the side as if he were listening to our conversation. I was sure he was onto us, but once the service started, Sylvia got into the rhythm of it and began to calm down a little.

"You can go up for Communion with me," she insisted, now much more relaxed. Her breathing had almost returned to normal.

I sat back and tried to get comfortable, but the pew was hard, and I had to keep shifting in my seat, so much so that my sitting bones were starting to feel raw. I tried to focus on the sermon, delivered by the older head priest, but my thoughts strayed to my friend and her obsession. The priest's message was simple enough. He was basically telling us not to be jerks and not to covet our neighbor's material goods, which is always good advice.

When it was time to get in line to receive, I followed behind Sylvia who conspicuously crossed over to the other side of the church where Father Tom was handing out wafers. Her transparency was obvious; she wanted to receive from the priest of her choice.

The older priest was working the other side of the church, and his line was made up of old women and men, while Father Tom's line seemed to hold a disproportionate amount of women under the age of sixty. Maybe Sylvia wasn't the only one with a crush on the hot priest.

Sylvia began breathing heavily again as we approached Father Tom. He dropped the wafer into her hand, making the most minimal contact of his skin against hers. I'd positioned myself off to her side so I could witness their encounter firsthand and take notes. Her face bore an intense look of adoration, as if she were witnessing the Blessed Virgin herself descending upon us. It was pretty bad.

"Did you see that?" she asked breathlessly, as we returned to our seats. "Did you see how his hand lingered on mine? He paused for a second. I *felt* it."

I shook my head, not sure whether to be brutally honest or to let her live in her fantasy world for a while longer. She had it bad for Father Tom. For her own good, I was going to have to try to figure out how to put a stop to it.

In retrospect, my comments were probably a little too harsh. Especially in light of the fact that Sylvia didn't speak to me for a week afterward, ignoring my friendly waves hello and letting my phone calls go directly to voice mail. But there's a time and place for make-believe. Where it doesn't belong is in terms of its application to real-life situations. I mean, what good is it for an emancipated woman of the twenty-first century to cling to the idea that one day, a prince on a white horse was going to ride up and carry her away? Or in Sylvia's case, a priest in a black cassock riding a donkey?

We left church right after Communion, not waiting for closing prayers. I'd had enough, plus there was the issue of Javier's waffles. This was my first mistake, not letting her go through the reception line at the end of the service to shake hands with Father Tom.

"Sylvia, I'm sorry," I said as we walked to her car, "but I will *not* support you in this behavior for one more second."

She glared at me as she punched her car's remote, wordlessly opening the door and bursting into tears the second she got in and sat down. The tears caught me off guard; I felt like a monster.

"You *don't understand!*" she yelled between sobs. "This is what I look forward to all week. This is what gets me through all of the crap."

She was working herself up, I could tell. I'd seen this kind of thing before, and I knew my best bet was to let her vent, get it out of her system.

"I've worked the same stupid job, I see the same stupid people day after day, for fifteen years. *Where* is the good in *that?*"

I handed her a tissue; she blew her nose, convulsing. It was sad, as if I personally had broken her heart, which I guess maybe I had. But sometimes the mark of a good friend is honesty. Isn't it better to tell someone what they need to know instead of letting them harbor false hopes? I took a deep breath for strength and laid this little bombshell on her:

"Look, there's something you should know about me, if you haven't picked up on this already. Love is something I'm serious about. It is *way* too important for life—I mean, so ridiculously important—that we should *not* waste our time on someone we don't have a shot at being with. A Catholic priest is one of those people, along with the President of the United States, or the King of England," I said, ticking the different choices off with my fingers as she listened. "All of those choices would be incorrect. So it's better that you get used to it not happening—I mean, get used to the idea right this minute—instead of wasting your life waiting for something that is *not* going to happen."

Maybe I shouldn't have raised my voice, but I wanted to impress upon her exactly how I felt.

She started the car and drove home in silence, not bothering to pull the car up into my driveway, instead parking in her own driveway. She got out, walked directly into her house and slammed the door behind her, at which point I walked across the street in silence, cursing my honesty.

Sometimes, I will concede, I may possibly need to choose my words a little more carefully, but I remain firm in the belief that every word I said was right and true. Even if she did hate me.

I said I was right, not smart.

Chapter Thirteen

I was starting to get used to the fact that my new normal involved Sylvia and I being former friends. Not really. But she was seriously pissed. And while I usually don't go out of my way to act like a jerk, apparently that was her current opinion of me.

Javier and I discussed the situation as we watched Matilda decorate the Christmas tree, putting twenty ornaments on the same poor branch, which was now hanging too low because of the extra weight. I knew I'd be rearranging them later after she'd gone to bed.

"Babe," Javier said patiently, "don't you think there's such a thing as being too honest?"

I reached for the wine, refilling our glasses, swirling mine before answering.

"But what does that achieve? How is indulging in fantasy doing someone a favor? *How* is it going to help her?"

"You're assuming she wants to hear the truth," he said flatly. "How often do people actually want to hear the truth?" he asked, his expression deadpan.

For an artist, Javier can be aggravatingly pragmatic at times, which annoys me to no end. I tried once more to defend myself. "Okay, so when your friends ask you for advice, do you tell them the truth?"

He said simply, "I don't give advice."

"Bullshit."

Matilda spun around to chastise me. "Mom. You're not supposed to use that word!"

"I'll put a dollar in the swear jar," I said with a fake smile, lying to my daughter. If I were to put a dollar in the swear jar every time I said a no-no word, we'd have enough money to take a trip around the world. First class.

"I don't," Javier said with a smug look on his face. "Seriously," he said in answer to my skepticism. "Correction. I don't volunteer advice. And guys don't talk about these things anyway."

Now, I *knew* that wasn't true. Men talk about women; men talk about men. Men were just as gossipy as women, and just as much in need of advice when it came to matters of the heart.

"So let me ask you something: if you don't give advice, then why do you always seem to be giving *me* advice?"

"That's different. You're my wife," he said dismissively. And annoyingly. I got up in a huff, left him sitting on the couch, and helped Matilda with the Christmas tree, trying not to think bad thoughts about my husband who, as always, was right.

After a week of Sylvia's serious case of cold shoulder, I found myself at the front door of the Cruz house with a container of frozen cookie dough in my hands, a peace offering from Matilda's latest school fundraiser.

Ofelia, her mother, answered the door, ushering me in. She was holding a red-and-white checked dish towel in one hand with another draped over her shoulder as backup. I could tell I'd caught her in the middle of kitchen duties, which seemed to account for at least fifty-percent of her time. The smells that come from her kitchen send me into serious flights of fantasy. I've often pictured myself as unfortunate orphan Oliver Twist showing up at her back door with a bowl in hand and pleading eyes.

"I'm sorry to interrupt."

The older woman waved me off. "Oh, we're just watching my stories." She leaned over and whispered, "Antonio's hooked."

Her husband sat on the floral-patterned living room couch, eyes fixed on the television.

"It's like eating popcorn," I said, "once you get started, you can't stop."

She laughed. "Let me tell Sylvia you're here."

I sat down next to Antonio to watch the Mexican soap opera. I knew enough of the words to know that the beautiful, young, large-breasted woman and her handsome young lover were involved in a scheme to kill her rich, old physician husband. Antonio gave me a wordless nod, too absorbed in his program to bother with conversation.

"Oh, and just *how* do they think they're going to get away with this?" I asked the TV. Antonio shook his head.

"Don't drink it," I yelled to the kind old doctor whose tea was poisoned with arsenic. The scheming lovers had been slowly lacing his tea with the poison. Antonio looked over at me, a little annoyed.

"Sorry."

Sylvia emerged from her bedroom.

"Hi, Julia."

Her expression was flat. She didn't seem happy to see me. I handed her my cookie-dough peace offering. "It's white chocolate chip macadamia nut."

"I'm not dressed for company," she said, without enthusiasm.

"Neither am I," I said, unwilling to back down.

Antonio glared at us; we were disturbing his *telenovella*. I hadn't been exposed to his grumpy side before; apparently he took his soap operas very seriously.

"Why don't we sit in the dining room," she said in a low whisper. "I'll make some tea. Should I put some of these in the oven?" She held the plastic pail of cookie dough up.

"Yes, you definitely should."

There was hope, at least for that part of me that wanted fresh, warm, baked goods.

We sat across from each other, at the end of the formal dining room table that was covered with a white lace tablecloth that Ofelia had crocheted. It was a remarkable piece of work, something I could never picture myself doing. Not in *this* lifetime. Sometimes I feel bad about being born without the crafting gene. I've always felt out of step with the women who scrapbook and create things out of little bits and puffs of nothing. Those were the *real* women, the ones who made do with what they had, like pioneers. I would totally suck it as a pioneer woman.

I held my cup of tea, warming my hands. Sylvia's eyes were downcast, staring into hers. We both spoke at once, awkwardly trying to fill the space with the right opening line.

"Julia, I'm sorry—"

"Sylvia, I just wanted to say—"

She held up her hand. "Let me do this. I'm sorry."

"You don't need to do that."

"No, I do. I overreacted, and I'm sorry. But I need to explain—"

I cut her off; I shouldn't have. "You don't need to explain anything."

"Are you going to let me talk, or not?" she said, her tone short.

"Sorry."

Sylvia wasn't usually so forceful, but it was about time she'd developed a backbone. Why she had to develop it with *me*, though, was the question. She sat across the table from me in her old maroon track suit, not a stitch of makeup on her face, chunky black glasses, hair pulled back into a ponytail. Her attitude and looks were both tired resignation.

"Look, I know this whole thing with Father Tom is crazy. I know that, but just *try* not having anyone to even dream about being with. When a person doesn't even have someone to *think* about, how sad is that?"

I nodded, biting my tongue. I didn't want to say the wrong thing and set her off. She was becoming hard to predict; I kept my cool.

"But you don't know what it's like, do you?" she continued.

"I don't know what what's like?"

She gave me an eye roll. "Look at you. You're pretty; you're funny. You have no fear of life. Have you ever not gotten *exactly* what you wanted? And if you haven't, didn't you go right after it until you did?"

That hurt. It's so easy to know someone else's life story, or to make one up for them.

"What about the whole: Don't judge a person until you've walked a mile in their moccasins?" I asked, indignant. "I'll pretend you didn't just say that, I mean, in the interests of not getting upset right now."

"Sorry," she said, not seeming all that sorry. "Okay, maybe that's not true, but you've got a great-looking husband, kid, home. The whole package. And here I am alone. Every night, every day, alone." She paused, her voice catching. "What if my parents weren't here? Then what?" she asked rhetorically.

I pictured her as an old woman sitting in a rocking chair in a cold, empty house, a few cats sprinkled here and there, and Raul. Her single older brother, in all likelihood, would be there too unless something drastic happened to change his life.

Maybe it wasn't a rhetorical question, though; maybe she *wanted* me to supply her with the answer to her life's problems. I paused, not wanting to blurt out something insensitive, but really, whose fault was it? Her parents'? Hers? Did it matter? I'd never gotten a good answer from Sylvia as to why she still lived with her parents at age thirty-six. My uneducated guess is it had something to do with Ofelia's wicked cooking paired with her homemade lunches. Oh, and the fact that Sylvia never had to do her own laundry. I pondered putting in my application and wondered if Ofelia would consider an adult adoption.

"Julia, are you even listening to me?"

"Sorry."

My adoption fantasies had taken me away for a few blissful moments. Sylvia gave a put-upon sigh and continued her complaining.

"You don't know what it's like to live day after day with no self-esteem. You don't know what it's like to feel ugly and invisible. People don't look at me. They don't *look* at me," she repeated. "If I disappeared, who would even miss me?"

She wiped at the corner of her eye, clearly in the throes of a world-class pity party, which was going to get her exactly nowhere. But her need was a universal one. Everyone needs to think that they're special in some way, and loved. I felt sorrow for her plight—the plight of so many poor souls out there in the world alone.

"So maybe it's time to change," I suggested as softly as I could.

"Easy for you to say," she said with a shrug.

"Maybe it is. But you're never going to get anywhere until you at least *try*." I pointed to my cup of tea. "Any way we could get something stronger in here? Like maybe some wine? For inspiration, of course."

"Of course," she said, then laughed; she'd cheered up a little.

She brought out a bottle of Cabernet and two short juice glasses, and I sat pondering how to fix her life, thinking out loud.

"We can start small. New glasses, for instance. And get rid of the ugly sweaters."

"Hey, I *resent* that."

"Come on. You need to *work* with me. For starters, let's have you *not* dress like an eighty-year-old woman. Let's do some advertising."

"What am I, a billboard?"

"Let the world know you're open for business."

"Whatever that means." She made a frowny face and downed half her glass of Cabernet.

"The track suits have to go too," I added, pushing my luck.

"Oh, come on," she growled.

I held my ground. "I never said this was going to be easy. Nothing in life worthwhile ever is."

She nodded; my words seemed to be sinking in. The oven timer went off. I followed her into the kitchen and kept up my strategy talk as she donned potholders and took the cookies out of the oven.

We had time. Her transformation was infinitely possible but would only become probable if she actually *cooperated* with me.

I left Sylvia's house that day slightly buzzed from the wine and cookies but even more resolved that I was doing the right thing. I made the decision not to tell Sylvia about Ted though. I didn't want her to get all anxious and begin to put up roadblocks. No, I decided to proceed with the transformation process and stick to the original plan of introducing them at our annual Cinco de Mayo/Birthday Party.

And if Javier didn't like it, he could suck it.

Chapter Fourteen

There are two types of people in the world, those who are inward-looking—the types who lead lives of quiet desperation, to borrow a line from Steinbeck—and those that aren't. The brooding, unhappy types spend most of their time unsatisfied with many things, including their level of happiness in comparison to the happiness of their neighbors, and whether they are or are not deep down inside a truly unlovable person. They wonder if such a thing as happiness even exists, and whether it is, indeed, part of man's nature to be content.

Then there are the outward-looking cheerful optimists. These types don't examine their lives very often, and when they do, they're almost wholly satisfied with what they see. It's that simple. No fuss, no muss. No long nights looking up at the ceiling in despair, no feelings of self-consciousness or negative self-talk.

Javier accuses me of being the latter, which is, admittedly, an oversimplification that I sort of resent. He, of course, belongs to the inward, sorrowful group. He broods because he's an artist who hasn't had a gallery show in three years. Why? Because his time is devoted to fulfilling customer orders at his shop. And he has a family now and must be practical. Also, because it is part of his nature. Luckily, my cheerful optimism balances his natural tendency toward the negative.

Why do I not inward look? Part of the reason is my naturally sunny disposition. When I was born, I came out of my mother's womb skipping. Literally skipping. I tend to not dwell on the endless garbage we all must wade through as part of everyday life. To focus on that can have the tendency of keeping a person up at night, and *what* is the point of that?

The other part may have something to do with the fact that I am the office manager of a medical supply company, which mainly involves keeping such ordinary objects as walkers, wheelchairs, and portable toilets in constant supply, and if I were to spend any significant amount of time pondering this situation, I would be driven to either hanging myself in my bedroom closet, or simple defenestration (i.e., the act of throwing one's self, or someone else, out a high window resulting in certain death).

Personally, I choose to wring as much happiness out of life as I can. I don't lie awake at night reviewing how I've failed myself. I prefer snuggling followed by eight hours of uninterrupted snoozing.

All of this brings me to Ted, who, like Javier, is most definitely an inward-looking, life-of-quiet-desperation type.

Now that we'd become new-old friends, he was turning out to be much more interesting than I'd realized. There's nothing like drinking too much, turning into a sloppy drunk, crying, crashing at someone's house, then being nursed back to health to cause a new friendship to be formed. In the weeks since Thanksgiving, he'd been to the fights with my father-in-law Frank, and a football game with Javier. Those facts taken by themselves were nothing short of miraculous. It appeared that Ted was slowly coming out of his shell. At least with the Hawthorne-Florez family.

I watched him from my desk as he fought with his mother. He'd put her on speakerphone so his hands could remain free to input numbers, and also so he could mimic shooting himself in the head by forming a gun with his thumb and forefinger. His phone calls with his mother often involved a mock suicide attempt on his part. Sometimes he'd use a noose around his neck depending on his mood. It was always funny—a classic "bit" of visual despondency.

He tapped away efficiently, playing verbal badminton with her. Bitsy was in full attack mode.

"Her parents go to church with us. They're very nice people, Ted."

"No, Mother," he said flatly.

"I don't see why you won't even give it a chance. What could be the harm?"

Her voice had a petulant tone now, as if their roles had been reversed and he was the father and she was the whiny little kid.

"No, Mother," he repeated, tapping the space bar on his computer a few times. "And the harm would be me spending an evening with complete strangers when I could be at home relaxing with Lord Byron."

I've always thought it was odd when people call their mothers "Mother." It sounds so Norman Bates-esque, cold and remote. I sometimes wondered if Ted hated his mother. I mean, at least as much as I did. And I didn't even know her, but I actively disliked the way she bossed and nagged him. It was very emasculating and shrewish.

"They've gone to the trouble of inviting you for dinner. It would be rude not to go."

Her voice had a pleading tone now, more reasonable, less forceful, like she was holding out hope that he'd make a deal with her.

"And you went to the trouble of setting it up without my consent. No, Mother," he said simply, with a tap, tap, tap of the space bar.

The conversation was going nowhere, so I went back to filling orders before I actually stuck a fork in my eye.

He ended the call and sat rubbing his temples as if he were trying to rub his headache away by sheer force of will.

"Rough call?"

He nodded. "My mother…" He trailed off to nothing. He sighed and mimicked plunging a dagger into his ribcage; I laughed. He's actually kind of a funny guy when he wants to be.

"Say no more. Let me buy you a cup of coffee," I offered. My work was almost caught up. Our boss Roger was playing a few rounds of golf. It was Friday afternoon; things were pretty well set for the weekend.

"Sure," he said, a smile starting to form at the corners of his mouth. "My mom—"

"I know. It's okay. She wants the best for her little boy."

He gave me a dirty look.

"You know," I went on, "that's really all she wants is for you to be happy. She can't help it. Certain people seem to have this *need* to make matches."

"Huh. Why is that? I mean, is that a female thing?"

He seemed serious.

"You know, I have no idea. I mean, it's not something *I've* had any personal experience with," I said innocently as I picked up my purse. The lies came too easily; I was almost concerned with myself. Almost.

He grabbed his sport coat and held the office door open for me, always the gentleman, and we continued our conversation in the elevator on the way down.

"I wish she'd give it a rest," he confided, running a hand through his hair, giving him the look of a little boy whose hair was going slightly awry. Ted was dangerous. Not that I'd ever even *think* of cheating on Javier, but this guy was seriously good-looking. With his green eyes and strong chin, his single status made no sense. I was beginning to wonder if it was more than simple shyness. Could he be asexual? One of those people who doesn't have romantic feelings at all, for anyone? If so, that would be a major bummer.

For Sylvia, I hoped it wasn't true. For womankind, I hoped it wasn't true.

We sat at the Coffee Bean & Tea Leaf next door, I with my mocha, Ted with his half-caf cappuccino. The smell of French roasted beans and chocolate croissants was heavy in the air. I'd managed to grab a little table in the back, away from the crowd, so we could talk.

Any doubts I had of Ted being attracted to women were put aside as I watched him place his coffee order with the cute red-haired barista. He fumbled and stammered and silently kicked himself. Poor guy.

I approached conversation with him slowly, careful not to scare him off.

"Ted, we've worked together all this time, and I still feel like I don't know what makes you tick. There's so much about you I don't know."

He stirred his drink, blowing across the top a little before taking a sip. As always, and most likely with everything in his life, he was cautious. A soul mate for Sylvia without a doubt. If the two of them ever had sex—which was a huge leap of the imagination—they'd first wrap themselves in bubble wrap. *And* use two condoms. I wanted to reach across the table and shake him—shake all of the shyness and contemplation and caution out of him. But that's me. I'm horrible that way.

"Um, what did you want to know?" he asked, a little hesitant.

"Forgive me—Javier would kill me for asking this—but *why* don't you have a girlfriend?"

I shouldn't have said it. Or at least not at that precise moment when he was taking a drink, because my question caught him off guard, causing him to swallow the wrong way and have a minor coughing fit.

"I'm so sorry," I said, patting him on the back. "Breathe, slowly through the nose," I instructed.

I'd said it, the question I'd wanted to ask him for so long. I'd just blurted it out, throwing caution to the wind. Sometimes a person has to go for it—take the bull by the horns. And sometimes when that happens, it can cause the other person to almost choke to death.

"Are you okay?"

"Swallowed the wrong way," he said, between coughing spasms.

We sat quietly. He sipped; I sat feeling awkward and guilty. I pressed on.

"There's no reason for it, you know. You're a handsome, smart guy. You're funny too, in an oblique, quirky, odd sort of way."

He gave a self-conscious laugh and wiped his hands on his pants as if his palms were starting to sweat. I wanted to kick myself under the table, but since that was physically impossible, I forged ahead. Damn the torpedoes.

"I hope I'm not embarrassing you. I've been known to do that on occasion," I said, apologizing.

It seems like I'm always apologizing for something.

"No, no. You're okay." He sighed and took a sip of coffee. "I guess I've, uh, never been good with social situations."

Social = girls.

"You mean girls?"

"Yeah." He smiled, this time wider, less self-conscious. "My confidence goes right out the window. It's terrible. My mind goes blank; I lose my words. When I do manage to get the words out, it's always something stupid or wrong. Awkward. So somewhere I stopped trying. I gave up."

I sat across from him, nodding sympathetically. Poor lonely Ted. He looked so vulnerable, I wanted to hug him and tell him everything would be okay. Inside, I wanted so badly to tell him about my perfect friend: the beautiful, smart, shy, and wonderful gem called Sylvia, but I stopped myself. With all my strength, I stopped myself. In Ted's eyes, it would just be another setup. I had to play it cool, keep her on the down low.

We drank our coffees, nibbling the biscotti dipped in chocolate, and talked. Ted doled out little bits of information about himself incrementally, as if each little factoid about his life were a piece of treasure that he didn't want to part with. In other words, it was like pulling teeth. He told me about his childhood, how it felt to grow up in a wholesome Norman Rockwell-like suburb of Salt Lake City.

"I was the only non-Mormon kid on our block," he said with one of his characteristic weak half smiles, which caused me to want to hug him again, but I resisted the impulse. Sometimes I surprise myself with how very disciplined I can be.

"Ouch. A little awkward, was it?"

He nodded. "It was. Mostly lonely though," he confessed. "Plus, there's the whole thing about my mom being neurotic and crazy."

"Don't feel bad; my parents are crazy too."

"No, I'm serious. Try being the one kid different from everyone else. And my mom truly is crazy."

I pictured poor Ted growing up awkward and alone, the classic last kid picked for the baseball team scenario.

"Dude, that sucks."

He laughed and kept talking, opening up a little more, expanding on his bleak worldview.

"It feels like it's not going to happen for me, so I've kind of resigned myself to living with my cat. One day, when my parents are older, I'll probably move back home and take care of them. I'll find another accounting job, and maybe, if I'm very lucky, I'll spend my retirement years living in a villa on the coast of Italy. Tuscany would be nice."

"Dude, that sucks," I repeated for comedic effect. He laughed again. "I'm sorry, Ted, but your life sounds like a Russian novel. It's like I'm reading Solzhenitsyn or Dostoevsky. Long winters, black nights, endless snowdrifts, adultery, suicides. Except for the part about Italy. Keep that."

"I guess I'll have to start drinking more. I'll write sad poetry," he said with a smile.

"And you can wear a little beret."

"Hmm. Do you think I could pull it off? I've always felt I was more of the boater type."

"Oh, you were born to wear a boater, darling."

I'd managed to make him smile a little, cheering him up a bit. The coffee shop crowd had thinned out. We'd been sitting there for half an hour, and its only other occupants were a group of students tapping away on their laptops. Ted was an enigma. I tried to wrap my mind around how he could be so resigned with his situation; how settled with life he was. I gathered my thoughts, and tried again with my pep talk, hoping to boost his shaky self-confidence.

"Listen, Ted, right now, as we speak, the Earth is orbiting in a vast universe where we are but specks in the grand scheme of things. Our lives pass by in the blink of an eye." I snapped my fingers for emphasis. "One day, we wake up, and we're old; life is over."

"And this is supposed to cheer me up *how?*" His eyebrows were raised, questioning.

I shook my head; he didn't get it.

"Which means we have to seize the day, *bro.*" I was waving my hands in the air now, working myself up, trying to make my point. "We've got to grab hold of life while we can. You've got to, before it's too late, Ted."

"Look, Julia, I wish it were that simple," he said, shaking his head. "Not everyone can be like you."

There was the comparison again. The same one Sylvia had brought up.

"Like me how?" I challenged. "Like me in that I'm friendly? I talk to people?"

"I mean how you're not afraid of things, like life," he said, almost apologetically. "It's not a bad thing. In fact, it's admirable."

He dipped his biscotti in his cappuccino, munching quietly, watching for my reaction.

"It's because I'm not an inward person," I said simply.

"Well, I think that's obvious," he said with a laugh. "I mean, I don't think anyone would accuse you of being a shy wallflower."

"True. I don't subscribe to the whole Socratic notion of an unexamined life not being worth living. My theory is the opposite: too much examination will cause a person to be filled with self-doubt, self-recrimination, *and* self-loathing."

"Or not enough self-examination can cause a person to be a complete ass and an idiot. There is that," he said, looking the tiniest bit smug.

I hate it when people get all reasonable on me.

"Refill?" I offered.

"Let me get it this time," he said.

"Okay, but do me a favor." I leaned forward in my chair for emphasis. "Say at least one thing to the barista that isn't about your order. Give her a compliment. Tell her you like the way she fixes your cappuccinos, how she gives you just the right amount of foam. Dig down deep inside. You can do it," I said, urging him on. "I mean, what's the worst thing that can happen? This is your first assignment. And I promise, you won't die."

He sighed and got up to place our order with the cute barista who wore a delicate ring in her nose and had long fingernails painted black. I'd seen her with her girlfriend and knew there was no chance she'd actually be interested in my handsome, socially awkward friend, but it was good training, and my evil plan would remain in place.

He returned with our drinks.

"How did it go?"

"Uh, swing and a miss? Do you have a shovel so I can dig myself a hole?"

"Hey, you did it. Now, was that so hard?"

"Yes. Yes, it was," he said with the barest hint of a smile.

Ted was toast. Luckily, though, I use my powers for good. Mostly.

Chapter Fifteen

"Go get a sample. Go on. He won't bite. I promise."

"How can you be sure of that?"

Sylvia seemed skeptical.

"Go."

I was urging Sylvia—literally pushing her—toward the two younger men behind the counter at the World of Hemp stand which was strategically situated between the kettle corn concession and the Texas Doughnuts booth at the Saturday farmers market.

As with Ted, I was trying to get my girl socialized, used to talking to members of the opposite sex, scary as that sounded. We were taking baby steps, but the farmers market was full of different kinds of people, from all walks of life. Opportunity was everywhere.

I kept pushing Sylvia, shoving her forward with little nudges.

"Do you mind?" She turned her head around and snapped at me.

"We've been over this. We agreed; you were on board with the plan. Time to put up or shut up."

"Okay, okay. All right. I've got this," she said in a focused voice, giving herself a little pep talk.

She smoothed her hair back, fluffed her bangs, took a deep breath, squared her shoulders, then immediately slouched back into her posture of resignation, slowly walking toward the hemp booth, not looking sure of herself at all.

The two men working the booth—both seriously handsome—were laughing with each other and seemed infinitely approachable. They were handing out samples of hemp milk, something I'd never heard of, but according to the promotional brochure I'd picked up and was browsing through, *everything* is made of hemp. Hemp is what makes the world go round and can be used to make everything from small boats to concrete blocks to clothing, which the two young men were wearing. I knew this because they had little stick-on badges that said "Everything I'm Wearing is Made From Hemp."

The young man with the beautiful eyes and tidy dreadlocks smiled at Sylvia, offering her the tray. She gave him a polite nod before taking a paper cup and sniffing its contents carefully.

"Tell me what you think," he said in a light accent that sounded vaguely French.

She put the cup up to her lips and looked over at me, unsure. I nodded, urging her on. Ever suspicious. She drank. The handsome young man wearing the hemp T-shirt bearing the words Free Your Mind waited for her reaction. She winced; he laughed; I was curious.

"Would *you* like to try?" he said, looking at me with a light smile.

"Yes, I would."

He offered me the tray.

"Cheers," I said, knocking mine back. Aside from its gray appearance and slight cardboard taste, it wasn't half-bad. Sylvia, resistant to all new things, simply had to get used to drinking plant milk.

"What's your name?" I asked the handsome young man who looked all of twenty-three or twenty-four years old.

"Paul. And yours?" he said, holding his hand out to me. I offered mine and he grasped it warmly.

"Julia. This is my friend Sylvia," I said, reaching over and tugging the sleeve of her hoodie, pulling her back to where I stood talking to my new Rastafarian friend. She'd been inching away from us slowly and hadn't said a word except for the occasional meaningful glance my way, her eyes urging me to leave. Clearly, she was out of her element. But, then again, most of the world was out of her element.

Paul viewed Sylvia with interest, studying her as though she were some strange new animal. He made an attempt to engage her in conversation.

"Well, Sylvia?" he said, his eyes questioning. "Did *you* like my milk?"

The wording seemed to throw her a bit. Maybe it was his command of the language, but I had to stifle a laugh.

"Uh, it was okay. It's different than what I'm used to," she finally managed in a barely audible whisper. Paul was leaning forward, straining to hear. She stood before him completely still, with a slightly panicked look on her face, like a cat caught in the middle of the road by a car's headlights. She fidgeted nervously with her purse, pretending to look for something inside.

Paul gave her a lovely reassuring smile and turned to me, asking the same question. "Julia, my milk—did *you* like it?"

I had a horrible vision of him being milked. I winced.

"It wasn't bad, Paul. But if I were you, I'd learn how to word that question a little differently. Just a bit of friendly advice."

Paul looked confused. His booth mate, who had been talking to another customer, overheard our conversation and let out a howl of laughter as Sylvia studied the collection of hemp shoulder bags emblazoned with giant marijuana leaves.

"Bro, I told you, don't say it's *your* milk. That sounds bad." He slapped his friend on the back and returned to his customer, an older man with a graying ponytail and Birkenstocks.

I tried again to engage Sylvia in conversation with the friendly but syntax-challenged hemp promoter, but she'd edged away from me again, this time browsing through the collection of water pipes.

"My friend here is looking for a gift for her mother," I said, lying.

Paul got up from his lawn chair and made a selection from the shelf.

"This one we have in the shape of a tulip. Maybe your mother would like it?"

Sylvia shot a hand up to her mouth, shocked at first then breaking out into a fit of giggles.

"Her mother's not a smoker, Paul," I said by way of explanation since poor Paul seemed confused. I pulled him off to the side and said quietly, "But maybe if you could talk to my friend a little, maybe show her around the booth, give her some ideas," I suggested.

He studied Sylvia again, taking a long look at her delicate profile and chunky glasses.

"She's shy, no?"

"She's shy yes," I said.

Paul rubbed his hands lightly; he seemed to have an idea.

"Perhaps you would like to go to the back and smoke with me? This would help her relax, no?"

It was an intriguing idea, one I'd never considered: Sylvia high. I thought about it for half a second before discarding the notion as a bad idea. It was too risky. And if her parents found out, I'd be banned from their home. Not to mention Javier, who would also ban me. Besides, the weed and I didn't get along so much. It had the undesirable effect of making me want to eat very large amounts of Cheetos *and* clean my bathroom. One thing it didn't do was relax me.

"No, Paul. I'm afraid that won't work. But you can wrap up that little green bong for me, if you don't mind."

It was delicate, and the little sign mentioned it could double as a vase. *Right*. But I did need a birthday present for Lisa.

My new friend, the hemp man, tried once more with Sylvia suggesting to her, "I have some very fine soap here, for the most beautiful skin."

"Oh. All right," she said quietly, touching her cheek, feeling it for smoothness. "I'll take a bar."

She smiled and handed him the five dollars.

"Do you come here often? Will I see you again?" he asked, flirting with her.

I watched Sylvia with eagle eyes, urging her on. Her face was drained of color; talking to a man was just that hard for her. She was all-but frozen up. It was really weird.

"Oh, um, not often. But we—I mean—uh, I think we'll be back again," she said loud enough this time for both Paul and I to hear her.

"I look forward to it," he said, his voice low, sexy.

I leaned over to Sylvia, whispering in her ear, "Now, was that so hard?"

"Yes."

She'd survived her encounter with a handsome stranger. Barely. There was hope.

"Oh, I'll take a half gallon of the hemp milk," I added.

My add-on order seemed to give Paul a big boost, an endorsement of "his" milk. Delighted, he surprised me by giving each of us a friendly, spontaneous hug.

"Goodbye then, ladies. It was my pleasure to meet you."

Other than almost being knocked out by the smell of ganga, Paul's hug was extremely satisfactory—soft and squeezy in all the right places. I watched with great interest as he hugged Sylvia, not giving her a chance to recoil. Her arms remained stiff by her sides as he enveloped her.

Baby steps.

In a small miracle, and a victory for the good guys, she found her voice after he released her from the hug.

"Thanks, Paul. It was nice to meet you too."

He beamed, giving me a wink.

"We'll see you later," I said.

"Come back sometime and we'll have a smoke," he said in a low voice, winking back.

"Sure thing," I assured him, giving him a friendly pat on the back, knowing it was not going to happen. Ever. Javier would most certainly not approve of his wife sitting around getting high with the guys from World of Hemp. Especially without him.

We walked away from the booth; I felt energized by Sylvia's response, giving her a squeeze of encouragement.

"That was good. Really good. You actually had a conversation with him. Awesome, dude."

I high-fived her; she high-fived me back.

"It wasn't bad, was it?" she said with a pleased-with-herself grin.

"Not bad at all."

We stood in line for kettle corn—the smell of sweet, greasy popcorn was too much to pass up—and I plotted our next move.

"See that guy over there?"

Sylvia's eyes followed my hand as I pointed to a man at the rock and mineral booth. He looked harmless, like he was maybe a high school biology teacher. He wore wire-rimmed glasses and a short-sleeved dress shirt with a pocket full of pens. He sat atop a stool surrounded by geodes and other semiprecious gemstones.

"I want you to go over to him and ask to see his rocks."

She gave me a sharp look. I was completely serious; I gave her a sharp look back. She sighed and we made our way over to the rock guy's booth to get some more practice in.

Baby steps.

Chapter Sixteen

Explanations are probably in order. I mean, a real, persuasive, solid reason why I'd remained so steadfast in my desire to bring Sylvia and Ted together, especially since I'd been questioning my very own motives. Like why couldn't I leave things as they were? Why couldn't I mind my own business for once in my life? Why couldn't the two of them go on with their lives—wretched, lonely souls that they were? I find myself asking myself a lot of questions. I rarely, if ever, have any good answers.

The roots of my incessant need to pair people up go back nearly thirty years.

When I was in the third grade, I made my first successful match. That it would prove to be my only *real* success to date as a matchmaker is something that has caused me a certain amount of disappointment. But I still remember the high I was on in the days surrounding the event. I can only liken it to the experience of a heroin user who describes the first time using as better than the best sex they've ever had in their life. The addict spends the rest of the time trying to recapture the feeling, but it eludes them just as the white whale in Moby Dick continued to elude Captain Ahab. I really should have taken the hint. But, then again, I'm not all that bright.

The "event" was my eighth birthday party, in which I had managed to wangle the attendance of my teacher, Miss Hunter, and the school's librarian, Mr. Steve, who had an unpronounceable last name with too many Ks and not enough vowels.

I'd noticed both were single and both possessed this sad quality about themselves, so much so that even at my young age, I'd picked up on their melancholy natures. During my class's weekly library time, one hour on Wednesday afternoons, I'd watch the two sad, lonely souls, adrift in their sea of loneliness.

Mr. Steve was handsome in a quiet way. He wore wool sweater vests over plaid ties, wire-rimmed spectacles, and had a mop of light brown hair. Miss Hunter wore wool sweater vests over Pendleton skirts, wore wire-rimmed spectacles, and had light brown hair that she'd pull back into a neat little ponytail. They were like two sides of a coin, and I believed them to be destined for one another. I'd watch as Miss Hunter would fix her hair, smoothing it into place and checking her lipstick before herding our class to the library, shushing us in her quietly firm voice. I'd watch, silently urging him on, as Mr. Steve became tongue tied around her.

Accomplishing the Herculean task of getting *both* of them to my party wasn't as hard as it sounds. I simply employed the mass-annoyance tactic. Every day for two weeks, I asked Miss Hunter if she was coming to my party. Every day for two weeks, I went to the library on recess and asked Mr. Steve if he was coming to my party. I invited every person, boys and girls, in my class to my party.

The day arrived; they showed. I was so excited, I practically turned cartwheels. The idea of their pairing was much more compelling than my party or the games my mother had planned for us. Mom kept pulling me back to musical chairs and pin the tail on the donkey as I watched Mr. Steve tentatively offer to refill Miss Hunter's punch. I was delighted when she laughed shyly at his jokes. It was clear they were completely smitten with each other.

They dated the rest of the school year, married when I was in fourth grade, and had a baby girl when I was in fifth grade. As far as matchmakers go, it was like hitting a homerun with three men on base. Definitely a hall-of-fame-level achievement.

That was my last successful match, and I've been trying to capture lightning in a bottle ever since. But love—real, true l-o-v-e—is a complex thing. I've spent many long hours thinking about the bits and pieces of things; the complexity of human interaction; personalities and emotions; temperaments; the knowns, the unknowns, and intangibles involved in two people coming together, and I've come to the conclusion that it's a small miracle any two people can put it all together and actually *find* love with each other.

Javier calls my compulsive need to bring people together my yenta complex. One conversation, he accused me of not receiving enough love as a child, which is untrue. My parents were and continue to be affectionate, huggy people. And I wasn't dropped on my head as a baby, that I know of.

Javier has also accused me of having selfish motives; in other words, the self-satisfaction I feel is my reward. When he does this, I want to poke him with a sharp stick. Luckily, the world is full of dreamers like me as well as the pessimists like Javier.

I've pondered the subject and questioned myself repeatedly, yet I'm still not sure why I do what I do. One thing I do know is that Sylvia and Ted will be my lighting in a bottle. I just have this hunch.

I mean, it could happen—right?

Chapter Seventeen

Javier and I sat outside the little beach shack on Pacific Coast
Highway, the place we drive so far out of our way to when we get
the overwhelming craving for fresh, line-caught tuna tacos. He
squeezed the lime over his plate, and I looked out over the
horizon. The winter sky was pink-and-orange swirls. The waves
crashed against the shore, and I pulled my coat close around my
neck. Matilda played with her food, which wasn't fish tacos. She
nibbled her French fries, and I took Lisa's call when I saw her
number pop up on my phone, apologizing to Javier.

"I'll make it quick," I promised.

"I need Ted's number," she demanded.

"Um, hello? Do I know you?"

"I'm serious. I need to talk to him. We have unfinished
business." By the tone in her voice, not warm and fuzzy, I
suspected she might be slightly deranged or that she'd been
drinking, and there was *no* way she was getting Ted's number.

I hadn't prepared for this. The chattering monkeys inside my
head were battling each other. One said, "Give her the number;
let the chips fall where they may." The other said, "What if she
ruins him? What if she takes our lovely, shy Ted and turns him
into a shadow of his former self? How will he survive?"

The second monkey made the decision for me. I'd lie.

"I don't have it."

"What do you mean, you don't have it?" she snapped. Her voice was like the Wicked Witch mixed with a little bit of Cruella De Vil, and she scared me a little, to be honest.

"He just changed his phone, and I didn't write the new number down. I'll get it tomorrow," I promised again, lying again. The lies kept coming, too easily. "Listen, we're in the middle of dinner. We'll talk later."

I put my phone away and smiled sweetly at Javier, who had stopped eating to listen to our conversation. He had that suspicious look on his face, the judgmental one I find so annoying.

"What?"

"Something's going on with you," he said with narrowed eyes. His eyebrows were knitted together. He was Detective Florez, all business. I waited for him to pull his notebook and pen out and start cross-examining me. "What's going on?"

"It was Lisa. She wanted Ted's number."

His eyebrows were raised now. "Huh." He went back to his tacos, took a few bites, swallowed. "Ted and Lisa. Huh," he repeated. "Do you think that's a good idea, babe?"

"Please, Javier. Think about what you just said."

He finished his beer, getting all philosophical on me. "Something I've learned in life is that you can never tell when two people are going to make a love match. Sometimes two people who seem nothing alike end up happy together." He wiped his mouth with his napkin and cleared his throat. "Compatibility is not always outwardly obvious."

"A 'love match'? 'Compatibility'? Seriously?"

He'd been hanging around me too long. He looked at me evenly and said, "Who are we to know these things? It's like playing God, or matchmaker."

There was that look again. I wanted to reach over and thump him on the head, but I refrained.

"Well," I said very patiently, "what I do know is that Lisa and Ted are a bad idea. And I can't believe you'd even suggest there might be a possibility of them getting together."

The thought of my father-in-law handcuffed to Lisa's headboard flashed through my head; I gave an involuntary shudder, thought about telling Javier, knowing at the same time what a bad idea it would be, then discarding the idea. I didn't want to scar my poor husband for life. The chattering monkeys were battling in my head again. Javier had been talking; I heard him midstream.

"Give her the number, don't give her the number. I have no opinion."

Yeah, right. When it came to matters of the heart, Javier was every bit as interested as I was, he just didn't want to admit it.

For the moment, I chose *not* to give Lisa Ted's number.

Chapter Eighteen

Help me. It's not an emergency, but help.

This was the somewhat cryptic text I received from Sylvia. I was in the middle of a game of Chutes and Ladders with Javier and Matilda when I heard my phone's buzz. I texted her back, intrigued.

What's wrong?

Thirty seconds later, she sent this: *I'll call you.*

We'd finished our game, since a complete game of Chutes and Ladders takes about ten minutes. Javier won. He says he's trying to get Matilda used to being a good sport about losing, that we shouldn't always let her win, but the truth is, he's very competitive.

Sylvia called.

"What's going on?" I asked.

"It's my parents. They're trying to set me up with a frog." She was whispering frantically into the phone.

Frog. Interesting. A picture of Sylvia walking hand in hand through a flowery meadow with a frog prince flitted through my head.

"Where are you?"

"I'm hiding in the bathroom," she whispered.

"You've got to give me more information. A frog?"

It was a very curious situation. She obviously didn't mean a literal frog. The fairy-tale joke possibilities were clearly there, but I restrained myself since she was in a serious mood and probably wouldn't take any attempts at humor very well. Most likely she meant that a man whose appearance closely resembled an amphibious creature was present in her home. I wondered if he had a low croaky voice and jowls.

Javier and Matilda were watching me, listening to the conversation. Intrigued. I tried to explain.

"It's Sylvia. Apparently she's got a thing going on with a froggy guy," I said, holding the phone away from my face for a second. They still seemed interested; both wore confused expressions. I shrugged my shoulders. "I'll have more details later, I promise."

"Why is Sylvia dating a frog?" Matilda asked her father, who was shaking his head, muttering, "This is why I've always said, fix-ups never work."

It was funny how he felt like he had to weigh in on this topic even when no one was asking his opinion. And a little judgmentally, if I may say so.

"You've got to get me out of here," she whispered, pleading.

"Okay. Give me a few minutes to think of something. I'll be there soon."

"Okay. 'Bye."

I racked my brain for several seconds before coming up with an idea.

"I'll be back in a few minutes," I said to Javier and Matilda as I grabbed my purse and headed out the door. "Most likely, with Sylvia."

I hurried across the street and rang the doorbell. As I waited, I hummed that obnoxious song, the one all over the Internet featuring the adorable cartoon cat and a rainbow, that I hadn't been able to get out of my head. For someone in such a hurry to escape, she certainly was taking her time answering the door.

"Julia, what a surprise," Antonio said, greeting me. "We were just having dinner. Come in."

"I'm so sorry to bother you, Mr. Cruz, but I have a little emergency. I was wondering if I could borrow your daughter."

He frowned—I'd interrupted their evening plans—but invited me into their home, being the gracious host that he was. The smell of carnitas, sautéed onions, and chiles was thick in the air, reminding me I hadn't had dinner yet. I *really* wished I could pull up a chair to the table and bring leftovers home for my poor hungry family. I also wished to have a secret adoption in which Ofelia would be my mother for mealtimes only.

I followed Antonio into the dining room where he quickly introduced me to their guests whose mouths were full of food. Pork carnitas—much better than the tofu patties my mother makes.

"Julia, this is Esther and Manny, old friends of ours, and their son Nacho."

"Hello." I gave a little wave. "I'm sorry to burst in on you," I said, apologizing. Sylvia was already out of her chair; her mother and brother Raul stayed seated. I started talking fast; I figured there would be less of a chance of my story not making sense if I spoke quickly. "I've got to run Javier to the emergency room, and, Sylvia, I need you to come stay with Matilda. I hate to disturb your dinner; I just don't want Matilda waiting in the ER with all of the gunshot victims and whatnot. You know, it's better she stays home. But we've really got to dash out of here. Sylvia?"

Our eyes met; Sylvia was silently thanking me with hers, I could tell. Her parents seemed disappointed, their plan foiled.

That's what you get for trying to set up your daughter, I thought to myself. Apparently the irony of the situation was completely lost on me.

After convincing Mr. and Mrs. Cruz that Javier wasn't in danger of imminent death but merely needed a few stitches in his hand due to an unfortunate kitchen-chopping incident, I ran out of their house followed closely by Sylvia.

"Oh my God. Thank you. Thank you," she said, practically tackling me in a bear hug, which was very out of character. She looked pretty. Her long hair was brushed out, falling around her shoulders, and she'd put the littlest hint of eye shadow and lip gloss on. The glasses were still way too severe for her face, but she was definitely on the upswing with her makeover-in-progress.

"Don't worry about that. Just get in the house. I'll drive around the block and sneak back in. You know, so it looks we've gone to the hospital."

"Wait. I'll go with you. It's dark. They won't see us, only the car."

We got in my car, and I drove around the corner, pulling up to the curb in front of someone's house, and parked.

"What are you doing?"

"Sylvia, we can't leave my car in the driveway. If they look out the window and see it there, they'll know something's up. We'll leave it here, then I'll sneak back and get it later."

She nodded. I'm always thinking.

"You've done this before, haven't you?" she said, impressed.

I had. I really had. Well, not this exact thing, but something like it.

"You make it sound so sinister."

"No, no judgment," she said, judgmentally. I could tell by the tone, that slight catch in the voice that says a person has spent too much time with nuns wielding rulers in case of shenanigans and not enough time left to their own devices.

How is a person supposed to grow up, living protected in a hot house?

We walked close to the curb, since there was no sidewalk, and crunched the pebbles in the asphalt. I hadn't brought a jacket, and it was cold out. I walked quickly; Sylvia struggled to keep up. The heels on her boots were too high.

"Wait up. My boots are killing me," she complained.

"New?"

"Yes." She sighed. "I bought this outfit yesterday after work." She was referring to her new black jeans and V-neck sweater.

"Cashmere?"

"Yes."

"Well, it looks great. The green brings out the color in your eyes. It contrasts nicely with your hair."

"Thank you."

"It was very considerate of you to buy a new outfit for your date."

I was trying to be funny. She didn't laugh. We took a few steps, walking side by side in the cold night air, and she dropped this little bomb on me, confessing, "I bought it to wear to Mass."

Her voice was wistful. I didn't mean to let out such an audible sigh, which was maybe more of a loud groan, but I did.

"Ugh."

"What?" she asked.

"Nothing," I said, shaking my head. What could I say?

"I know what you're thinking," she said, suddenly sounding a little bit defensive.

"Sylvia, what it sounds like you're telling me is you're trying to attract your priest, drive him wild with desire so he'll—what? Leave the church? Declare his undying love for you during confession? I mean, I'm just a little bit confused by your behavior. And isn't it wrong? Won't you burn in Hell or something? It's a little effed up, don't you think?"

I watched my breath swirl around me in little puffs. Sylvia was a gorgeous woman, especially now that she was beginning to let the world in on this little secret, but the fact remained: she was in love with her priest. It was a desperate situation.

"Julia, could we not talk about that right now?"

I nodded. No need to make her feel worse than she already did.

"Okay. Change of subject. So what's the story? Tell me what I'm rescuing you from. Or whom?"

"Or what," she said with a little laugh followed by a very audible sigh of resignation. "My parents tried to set me up with Nacho. He's the son of their old friends. I haven't seen him since I was a kid."

"Dude, your parents set you up with a frog who's named after food?"

"Stop calling me 'dude.'"

"It's a term of endearment. I'll call you 'bro' instead. How's that?"

"Dude's better. Anyway, it's short for Ignacio."

"Of course. I should have known." My quick thirty-second appraisal of Nacho revealed an older man by at least eight to ten years, with bulgy cheeks, no visible chin, and saggy neck skin. The skin around his sad brown eyes gave him the drooping look of a bulldog. In fact, he was more of a cross between a dog and a frog. He was probably a very nice man, but he was not a match for Sylvia.

We reached my house, but before we went in to join my family, Sylvia paused. "You know the worst thing about this?"

"Erm, no. What?"

"The very *worst* thing is that my parents tried to set me up without even consulting me first. How can they think so little of me?"

Poor thing. She seemed so depressed, and dejected.

"Hey, maybe it wasn't them at all. Maybe it was Nacho's parents."

I turned the knob to go in; she put her hand on my shoulder to stop me, her face was a mixture of pain and sheer befuddlement, as if she were trying to process the evening's events and implications.

"Wait. It's even worse than that."

"Worse how?"

She stared into my eyes and said in an even tone, "The worst part is he didn't even seem interested in me."

Poor Sylvia. It was time to start drinking.

We found Javier in front of the stove melting butter for the Alfredo sauce in one pan with water boiling in the stockpot. Matilda wore her frilly pink miniature cook's apron and was happily playing with the can of ready-made dough, shaping what were supposed to be crescents into oddly shaped lumps. Javier would have to adjust the baking time for *those*.

"Don't mind us, we're looking for the wine," I said.

"Are you joining us for dinner?" Javier asked Sylvia mid-stir, ever the polite host.

"No, don't mind me. I'll just make myself quiet while you eat," she said.

"Maybe you can teach Julia how to do that," he said. I caught his little devil smirk. That's when I gave him a quick smack to the top of his head; he totally deserved it. Then I instantly felt bad and kissed the back of his smooth bald head, which is very nicely shaped and not full of wrinkles from fat rolls like some of the bald heads I'd seen around town.

"You should be nicer to me," I whispered in his ear. He swatted me away.

"I'm cooking, woman."

Javier's well aware of the fact that his kitchen skills give him extra latitude; he's forever taking advantage of my culinary weakness, and he knows I'm willing to put up with a lot when food is involved.

Sylvia sat in one of the kitchen chairs as I set the table for four and poured wine in three glasses, taking a chair beside her.

By the way she was slumped in her seat, I could tell she needed cheering up, so I decided not to revisit the subject of Father Tom, hot priest, and instead opted for friendly conversation, which as it turns out, she wasn't so receptive to.

"So how's work?"

"Work's work," she said simply before continuing her brooding.

And…that took care of the main part of her life. There were only two other parts of her life: family and church. We'd already discussed church. No need to revisit *that* ground. And family—specifically, her parents—were low on her list of things to be happy about.

I toyed with the idea—played around with it in my head seriously for a few seconds—of calling Ted and spontaneously inviting him over. I pictured him alone in his apartment with his cat and a ball of yarn, another Saturday night at home, and then shook myself. *What was I thinking?* I had to play it cool with Ted, not blow it by releasing the balloon too soon.

"Have you considered women? I mean, as an alternative?" I said, making idle conversation, wanting Sylvia to make sure she'd explored her alternatives to Father Tom.

The look on Javier's face was funny. Matilda didn't get it. Sylvia did, though, and considered it for a couple of seconds.

"You know, I've thought about it, of course. That's not me though," she said, shaking her head.

"Hmm. Too bad."

We were starting to run out of options. And the doorbell rang.

"Were we expecting anyone?" Javier asked, about to throw a large handful of fettuccini into the pot.

"Wait. We might be adding another plate," I said. Meal times tended not to be set in stone in our house, partially, I'd come to learn, as a result of having a skilled cook in residence. Also due to the fact that Javier and I are both delightful *and* irresistible.

I opened the door to Lisa, who looked surprisingly forlorn. There must have been something in the air, something that was causing the single women I knew to hold their lives up to scrutiny and get all depressed about what the scrutiny revealed. She was bundled in a man's overcoat and baseball cap, uncharacteristically gray and drab, nary a stiletto in sight. It had been years since I'd seen Lisa in flats let alone tennis shoes.

"Got a minute?" she asked meekly.

"Come in. Of course."

She gave the air a couple of sniffs. "I'm not interrupting dinner, am I?"

"Mmm, not yet, but you will be." Because the look on her face was that of crestfallen dejection, I quickly added, "I can put in a good word with Javier, if you want. What's wrong?"

"Oh, nothing," she said, obviously fronting.

"What's with the shroud? You're a vision in pathetic."

"I need company right now," was all she said. I stepped back, surprised by this admission. Lisa was not one for showing weakness of any type. She never needed anything or anybody. Or if she did, she had a good way of hiding it. I couldn't remember the last time, if ever, she'd seriously asked for help.

"Follow me. Look sad," I whispered, and we proceeded to the kitchen to work our collective charm, which at this point was sketchy at best. Lisa approached my patient, long-suffering husband with her hands clasped in prayer, two large puppy eyes, and a downturned mouth. The whimpers were a nice touch.

"All right. Sit down," he said, as he threw an extra handful of fettuccini into the pot, and I introduced my oldest friend to my newest friend.

"Lisa, this is Sylvia. Sylvia, Lisa."

The two checked each other out like two strange dogs deciding whether to be friendly or not.

"Hello, I'm Lisa, and I'm totally depressed. How about you?"

"Sylvia, and I'm hiding from a frog."

The two shook hands. It seemed to be going well enough.

Lisa turned her full attention to my daughter.

"Miss Matilda, how have you been, little mama?"

Matilda ran over to her auntie from where she was working the dough at her countertop space, and gave her a long look.

"Why do you look so funny?"

"Auntie Lisa's in the middle of a depression," Lisa said, referring to herself in the third person. My five-year-old daughter didn't know about such adult things as depression and said nothing, instead tilted her head to the side, studying her.

"I'm making rolls," Matilda announced.

"I don't eat bread. Bread makes me fat. And sad," Lisa announced back.

Matilda was even more confused.

"Uh-oh," I said to Javier who was opening another bottle of Merlot. "It's going to be an interesting night."

"Well, I'm outnumbered. I think I'll take my dinner and hide."

That was funny. Javier likes to pretend he doesn't want to hang out with me and my friends, but he secretly loves it. He listens to everyone complain about their boyfriends and their diets, the latest gossip, and he offers the man's perspective every so often while they hang on his every word.

I took a seat at the table, watching the two women, trying to get a handle on them, while Javier fussed over our plates, grinding pepper and shaving Parmesan onto our pasta. I caught Sylvia gazing at him, practically swooning.

"Do you like what you see?" I asked, my sarcasm unveiled.

"You're so lucky," she said and then heaved a big sigh.

True.

"I want what you've got," Lisa announced simply. Javier ate it up with a spoon. Beaming. His head was big enough as it was without them adding to it.

"What do you mean?" I said to Lisa, intrigued. "*You* want a husband and kids? Seriously?"

"Yes. I've decided."

My mouth must have been hanging open.

"You're going to catch a fly, my dear," Javier said. "And *why* should it be so surprising that your friends think I'm such a catch? I'm a little offended actually," he said as he removed his apron, hung it on a hook next to the stove and sat down with us.

"Oh, that's not why I'm surprised. It's just I thought I heard Lisa say she wants to settle down, and have a family."

My old friend, distressed-looking and at her most drab, nodded. "I do. I'm serious."

I thought my words over carefully and tried to be nice about it, encouraging but not too encouraging. "Why don't you start small, like maybe get a goldfish first?" I suggested helpfully. She made a face.

"Goldfish? What do you think I am? Totally useless?"

"Not totally."

She made another face. I know, maybe it was harsh, but she'd never taken care of anything besides herself, and even *that* was doubtful.

"Motherhood's a pretty big step," I said, gesturing my head toward Matilda who sat playing with the long strands of fettuccini, feeding them to Dave, who sat quietly at her feet pretending to be invisible. "Um, your lifestyle would have to, um, adapt a bit. Don't you *think*?" I emphasized the last part, again gesturing my head toward Matilda.

"What's wrong with your head, Mommy?"

"Oh, nothing. Just eat your food."

Sylvia looked confused as well; she had no idea that Lisa had a unique relationship with men; that her apartment was basically a sexual playground, complete with swing.

"Well, I'm sick of being alone," she said simply. Her countenance changed; she was now sad. Her shoulders slumped; she threatened to completely bring down our collective mood.

"Oh." I glanced at Javier whose expression bordered on shock, but he remained silent. "Would you pass the wine, dear?"

He handed me the bottle, and cleared his throat. Lisa turned to look at him. "Was there something you wanted to say, Javier?"

"Yes, actually, if I could bring the male perspective into the conversation."

The room became quiet as we turned our attention to him and whatever pearls of wisdom he had to offer. He cleared his throat again, seeming a little nervous now. When Lisa turns her attention to someone, it can be a bit humbling, staring into her intense green unblinking cat eyes.

"Well, have you ever thought that sometimes you come across a little strong with men?"

"Me? Too strong?" she said, with voice raised in a strong manner.

The notion was shocking, to Lisa, not to any *other* person living on planet Earth.

Javier and I exchanged glances across the table; I gave a little shrug.

He cleared his throat and started again. "Men like to feel the woman they're with needs to be taken care of a little. A man, to feel like a man, has to be able to take the lead. At least once in a while."

Lisa's mouth was wide open. Sylvia was quiet, silently eating her fettuccini, getting an education. I braced myself for the certain onslaught.

"That is total BS, Javier. We live in a male-dominated society as it is. I'm sick of automatically giving men the upper hand."

And...she was back. Her arms were crossed in defiance. Javier looked up to the ceiling, gathering his thoughts.

"Look, I'm just giving you the male point of view," he said, patiently.

"Um, have you ever thought of women?" I tried using the same line I'd used on Sylvia earlier.

"Oh, sure. Of course. You know me." She waved her hand dismissively. "Being with a woman is like—well, it's like being with a woman! Too much talk about makeup and hair and clothes. Girlie things," she said with obvious contempt. "They get upset at the slightest thing—too many clothes left on the ground, or 'Why didn't you put the dishes in the dishwasher away?' You know, that kind of crap."

Lisa was funny; I considered the circumstances. One friend was desperately in love with her priest and had made a dramatic escape from an evening at home with a frogman. The other friend kept men in line for a living and wore black leather as a work uniform yet was suddenly in search of a family and complete lifestyle change, but *only* if she could remain in complete charge of things.

I took a quick inventory and counted wine bottles: two Merlot; one already-open cheap dessert wine for cooking. I took a deep, cleansing breath and braced myself. It was going to be a long night, I could tell.

Chapter Nineteen

Long after Matilda had been tucked in, long after Javier grew tired of listening to three adult women complaining about diets, periods, men, and all other womanly-related subjects, Sylvia, Lisa, and I sat around the kitchen table trading stories and drinking wine. It was *much* stranger than I would have expected.

"But I can't live without him. I can't," Sylvia complained, quite drunkenly. With at least three full glasses under her belt, she was gone. Her hair, which had been so neatly styled before, was now swirled about her face, messy. Her eye shadow had become smudged, somehow ending up under her eyes.

"What's your problem?" Lisa asked in her typical direct fashion. She was also drunk, but being a professional drinker, she was able to maintain. "Ask him out. What are you afraid of?"

"He's a Catholic priest," I said, as if that were enough of an explanation. I really should have known better.

"So what? Ask him out. He's a man; you're a woman. He's got a penis. I don't understand. *What is the problem?*"

"Lisa's never been to church," I said to Sylvia by way of explanation. "She's afraid she'll melt."

My old friend didn't dwell in the world of propriety and etiquette the way the rest of us did. She was far too pragmatic and actually preferred living the life of a man. And in some ways, I suppose life *is* simpler when you don't worry about what society thinks, when you don't adhere to the regular social norms and conventions. How freeing would *that* be? I considered complete abandon for a few seconds before returning to Earth.

Sylvia sat half-slumped in her chair, watching Lisa. Sylvia's face wore a confused expression, as if Lisa had two heads and silvery skin and was teaching a class on particle physics.

"You don't understand. I can't do that."

"Then stop it. Snap out of it and find someone else."

Lisa said this with authority. And she was right.

"She's right, you know," I said only partially drunk. "You'll get nowhere with him. Unless you plan on making a move, stop wasting your time. And ours."

The last part of what I said was mean, but I'd been drinking.

"So you're both against me now?" Sylvia said accusingly, evidently wounded.

I felt bad. She was now on the verge of tears and not used to how alcohol has a tendency to produce horrible emotional messy crying jags.

"I'll tell you what; I'll go with you when you ask him out. Or I'll do it," I volunteered, trying not to slur.

"Let's go now," Lisa suggested in a burst of inspiration, getting out of her chair. "We can walk there, can't we?"

In theory. We could have walked to St. Mary's under normal circumstances. For instance, if it weren't forty degrees out on a winter's night and if it weren't eleven-forty-five p.m. *and* if the Saturday evening service hadn't been over for hours. Oh, and also if we weren't in various stages of drunkenness.

But we didn't consider any of these facts because everyone knows that things sound much better when a person is drunk.

So, while three drunken women walking several blocks in the cold is probably never a *good* idea, there we went, out into the night. We were three unwise women with a half-baked nebulous plan that wasn't a plan so much as a vague notion of finding Father Tom and declaring Sylvia's undying passionate love and devotion for him. The fact that kidnapping him was discussed at all should have been a huge red flag.

But there we were.

"Wait. I forgot the wine."

Lisa ran back into the house while Sylvia and I shivered in the cold on the front porch, too full of alcohol to have the presence of mind to go in with her. She found the one bottle left that was three-quarters full. It was the cheap dessert wine —a Muscatel—that Javier used in his marinades and for deglazing messy pots and pans. Not something we'd ever dream of actually drinking.

"I got it!" she yelled, excited, before tipping the bottle up to her mouth, taking a swig and passing it to Sylvia who took a long drink and burst into giggles.

"Give me that," Lisa demanded, in control of the bottle again. They drank; we stumbled a few steps and managed to make our way down my driveway to the sidewalk in front of my next-door neighbor Doris's house. Her curtains rustled; she was watching us as we took our loud, drunken walk with Lisa in the lead and Sylvia close behind, fighting for the bottle.

It was freezing; I could see my breath clouding. Somewhere in my alcoholic haze, I remembered something. Something had happened earlier that evening *before* we started drinking.

"Sylvia, wait up," I yelled out to the night air.

She and Lisa were now wrestling over the cheap wine, with shy wallflower Sylvia reaching across Lisa's shoulder, grabbing for the bottle, and Lisa batting at her, attempting to swat her away.

The whole thing was getting to feel very much like a scene from *Lord of the Flies*.

"Wait. I'm not finished," Lisa growled, sounding a little bit like a mountain lion. There was a struggle then, with Sylva losing her balance—probably due to those new boots of hers with the heels—and slamming against Doris's Explorer. The car alarm's honking horn and flashing lights scared her.

"Oh crap. Crap."

In a panic, she inexplicably ran out into the middle of the street toward her house, falling twice. I watched it happen, right in front of my eyes, but it was all in slow motion. Then I remembered what it was I'd been trying to recall: Sylvia had escaped a strange froggy man and was hiding out at my house under false pretenses.

"Sylvia! Get over here," I yelled.

She'd made it halfway across the street, turned around and ran back.

"Wait for me," she cried out, gasping for breath.

The alarm was still blasting.

"Quick. Run!" Lisa bellowed. "Stop crying. Move," she barked at us, in command, her dominatrix skills taking over.

"Shit. My light's on," Sylvia cried when she saw the porch light turn on across the street at her house.

"Run. Run!" I was laughing. "Your parents are going to bust us."

"We'll have to go to detention," Lisa cried, smacking me on the rear end, howling with laughter.

We stumbled up the driveway to my house, falling into each other.

"You guys are so mean," Sylvia said, unhappy, before squatting down in the middle of my driveway for some reason.

"What are you doing?" I asked, curious. Foggy.

"I have to go to the bathroom."

"Oh, my God! Don't do that here!" I yelled as she started to fumble with the top button of her jeans.

My porch light flicked on. Javier was obviously on to us. Doris, in her bathrobe and curlers, was outside, car keys in hand, scowling at our sorry group as she punched the button on her remote.

"Oh, shit. We're busted more," Lisa said, laughing as if the whole thing were a big joke.

Javier came out to collect us in his pajama bottoms and T-shirt, disappointed with our behavior. I hung my head in shame.

"What's wrong with you, acting like teenagers? You're waking the neighborhood. Get in the house," he scolded.

"Quick, Sylvia. Get in there," I urged, before she relieved herself on our driveway.

She ran ahead, making it into the bathroom in the nick of time, and returned to the living room a few minutes later looking remorseful.

"I hate myself. I hate my life. No one loves me. I have no one," was her pitiful refrain. She threw herself on the couch, dissolving in messy makeup-stained tears.

When Lisa started to sniffle, I knew we were screwed.

"Don't you go south on me now," I warned her. Two women crying were too much for poor Javier. If Lisa started, I'd go next.

"I'm so lonely. You don't know how lonely I am. My life sucks."

Her eyes were downcast; she was working herself up.

Lisa was drunk and wretched; Sylvia cried. Lisa cried. I felt a tear, then two, slide down my face in solidarity.

After a few heaving sobs, pathetic Sylvia passed out on the coach, her arms and legs sprawled in all four directions like points of a compass.

Once again, I tucked Lisa into bed, but this time in our spare room.

Our house seemed to have become some sort of vortex for socially awkward individuals with little to no experience with alcohol and/or the opposite sex. And it felt like I'd brought it all on myself. I slid into bed next to Javier who kept his back turned to me, pretending to be sleeping. I felt his disapproval in the form of an invisible wall between us.

We never did make it to church that night; Father Tom remained where ever he was, unmolested—thank God for small favors—but we did succeed in ending the evening with the three of us dissolving into tears after our drunken walk of shame and regret.

So I guess the evening wasn't a *total* disaster.

Chapter Twenty

My mouth felt like cotton. Javier slept peacefully, the calm, restful sleep of the innocent and those who know better than to drink too many glasses of wine, get stupid drunk, and do wildly impulsive ridiculous things that you'll regret the next morning.

Somewhere in the far recesses of my mind, a bell was ringing, and it grew progressively louder. When the sound repeated several more times, I realized someone was at the door. I picked up the alarm clock on the nightstand and tried to focus on the fuzzy numbers that seemed to read seven-forty-five. In the morning.

Javier opened his eyes. "Someone's at the door," he mumbled. "Who's at the door?"

"I don't know," I mumbled, grabbing my robe and staggering out. Sylvia was still passed out on the couch; a puddle of drool had formed at the corner of her mouth. I peeked through the peephole and saw Antonio, fresh and handsome, wearing a sport coat and tie, silver hair combed carefully back, dressed for church.

Crap.

"Good morning, Julia," he said—bright, cheerful, and enthusiastic. All things I was not. "I tried calling Sylvia, but she didn't answer her phone. We're leaving for Mass in a few minutes."

"Oh, of course." My mouth was smiling while my brain had gone into panic mode. I tried to think of some way to excuse my friend. "I'll let her know," I said with a fake smile, and started to close the door. Antonio caught it with his hand.

"How's Javier doing?" he said, a look of concern on his kind, weathered face.

The lie. The *lie*. I'd forgotten all about it. Alarm bells were clanging against the hamster wheel in my head, which was giving me a big headache.

"Oh, he's doing just fine," I said with a little laugh to show Antonio that everything was perfectly fine; there was no cause for alarm. "He only needed a couple of stitches."

I'd completely forgotten about the nonexistent trip to the hospital, the frogman, and the priest. The whole thing seemed surreal in the cold light of day. And the lies continued to issue forth from my lips so easily, I felt guilty. Here I was lying to a sweet older man on his way to church. *God, please forgive me. Please don't strike me dead from the lies.*

This was a prayer I'd found myself saying a lot lately.

"Oh, I'm glad to hear it," he said, a relieved smile on his face, which made me feel even more like a heel. "Send Sylvia home, will you? We're leaving in ten minutes."

"Will do, Mr. Cruz," I said with false energy. "And say hello to Mrs. Cruz for me."

"I certainly will."

I watched him go on his way, cheerfully ignorant about the terrible goings-on of the night before, shut the door and went into full-on red alert.

"Get up. Get up. Get up." I grabbed Sylvia by the shoulders, shaking her. She grunted, swatting my hands away. "Get. Up!"

"Get away, asshole."

That was unexpected. I stepped back, stunned, put a hand up to my mouth, and laughed; I couldn't help myself. Sylvia had never, to my knowledge, used that word before. *Someone* was going through some sort of metamorphosis. *Someone* was growing a spine. I *liked* it.

"Sylvia!" I shouted into her ear. "Your parents are going to Mass in ten minutes. If you don't get up, your dad will come here and get you himself. Do you want that to happen?"

That did it. She opened both eyes and gave a low whimpery moan.

"Oh my God. What happened to me? Where am I? What did you *do* to me?"

She remained in a recumbent position, completely horizontal, flat on her back. Mass was most likely *not* going to be part of her Sunday reality as much as a raging headache and general all-over poopy feeling were.

"You drank way too much wine, tried to visit Father Tom somewhere just before midnight but fell into Doris's car instead. Her car alarm went off and Javier busted us. Now you have a hangover."

I tried not to smile as I said it, but I did. It was beyond ridiculous when I said the words out loud.

"I hate you."

"Don't shoot me, dude. I'm just the messenger."

"Where's my phone?" she asked in a whisper.

It was lying on the coffee table, not more than three feet away from her. I pointed to it; she made audible creaking sounds as she rolled her body over to reach it. After her first weak attempt, she gave up. I handed it to her; she looked at it as if it were a bottle opener and not a cell phone.

"Here." I grabbed it out of her hands and dialed her parents' number, handing it back to her. The lies continued, this time from her end. It was pretty heinous. I shook my head in judgment.

"Daddy, it's me. Yeah, I'm okay. No, you go ahead. I woke up with a headache. No, no. It's okay. I'm okay. All right, I'll see you later. 'Bye."

Well, it wasn't so much as a lie as an omission. The headache was certainly part of her Sunday reality. For sure.

She handed the cell phone back to me, as if putting it back on the table were too much effort, rolled back over on her side and went back to sleep.

I sat on the comfy red wing chair with my legs huddled around me, next to the sofa where my friend lay, sprawled out in all her glory. Matilda was stirring; my head was thick with fog. I braced myself for my daughter and the inevitable questions, like, "Why is Sylvia sleeping on the sofa? Why is Aunt Lisa sick again?" and hoped Javier didn't want to divorce me.

Another Sunday morning with hung-over friends. It seemed to be becoming a pattern. Don't they say in self-help manuals that part of realizing you have a problem is noticing a pattern of behavior developing? I contemplated this thought for two seconds before discarding it. Noticing the behavior developing is one thing; having the desire to change it is another.

Lies had been told; barriers had been lowered—Sylvia's— and vulnerabilities shown—Lisa's. I was still in shock over that one. While I sat replaying the evening's events in my head, Matilda toddled out in her Princess Ariel nightgown, followed close behind by Dave the dog, her nighttime companion.

"Why is Sylvia sleeping on the couch?" she said with wide eyes. Dave immediately made his presence known, pushing his very wet nose into Sylvia's face, not so gently nudging her. "Did you have a slumber party?"

Cute. A slumber party. She was so innocent.

"Yes, *mija*, I did. But let's be quiet," I said, putting a finger up to my mouth, "because they stayed up *way* too late, and you know how cranky Aunt Lisa gets when she hasn't had enough sleep."

"Aunt Lisa's *always* cranky in the morning," she said, adorably sincere. I gave her a hug and wanted to eat her up—all of her adorable five-year-old virtue. Little kids are so cute when they're still sweet and not jaded and too grown up. We snuggled in the wing chair and watched Tom and Jerry bash each other over the head with brooms and baseball bats with the television's volume on low, waiting for Javier to wake up and take pity on us. I was hoping for waffles.

Javier, in fact, did take pity on us and whipped up a batch of his famous blueberry pancakes. Matilda insisted on small mounds of whipped cream on top. The pancakes were like little bites of Heaven.

Sylvia's intermittent snores in the next room were punctuated by her other bodily noises which caused Matilda to giggle uncontrollably.

"What's wrong with her, Mommy?" she asked, her eyes wide with wonder.

"She's a little sick this morning," I said. Javier shook his head in disgust.

"Your friends. I swear."

"Please, no editorial comments. No need to go there," I said with a polite smile. "Besides, I've spent a few mornings with *your* friends." And I had. Plenty of mornings with his gang of ne'er-do-wells, not to mention a stray uncle or two. Javier had quite a few honorary uncles—Frank's interesting band of characters who'd helped raise Javier and his brother Rudy.

He held his hand up. "Say no more."

The Dragon soon emerged, with much wailing and gnashing of teeth, well into breakfast, which the three of us were enjoying in the sun-filled kitchen. I so love the quality of light on a winter's morning, bright white and clear. The Dragon, however, did not and shielded her bloodshot eyes as she stumbled into the kitchen still wearing her overcoat and baseball cap from the night before, hugging a blanket that she'd wrapped around her shoulders. Combined with the thick, knee-length, green wool socks I'd given her to keep warm, she looked perfectly ridiculous.

"It's too bright in here," she said, offended by the light.

"Good morning, merry sunshine," I said.

She glared at me most foully and took the seat next to Matilda, brushing Dave out of the way rather rudely to get to her seat. Javier shook his head and sighed.

"There was something about a priest last night. We were going to find one?" she said, trying to grasp the events of the night before, which were sketchy for me as well. "Why was there a priest?"

Javier looked over at me, also confused. I shrugged.

"So maybe that wasn't our *best* idea," I said, by way of a non-explanation.

Lisa sat, quiet; Javier got up from his seat and placed a large mug of hot coffee in front of her. She grabbed hold of it as if it were her cure, holding on for dear life.

"Why was there a priest?" she repeated, still trying to reconstruct the night before.

"Well, the priest represents Sylvia's notion of romantic love. Father Tom is unobtainable, and she knows this, so we were going to kidnap him. I think."

I said it as a joke. Matilda, who never seems to be paying attention, but almost always is, chimed in with her disapproval. I *really* should have known better.

"You were going to kidnap a priest?" Her eyes were as wide as silver dollars.

"No, no, no. I'm just joking. No, *mija*, we were having fun."

Javier shook his head, something he seemed to be doing a lot of lately. Lisa shook her head as well, but for a different reason.

"She should just ask him out and get it over with."

I looked at her as if she had rocks in her head.

"Okay, one: that will never happen. Two: she's not really in love with him. He's her proxy relationship—her safe crush. This is what she does. Over and over again. Her past is littered with crushes. Father Tom is her dream guy. She has no intention of doing anything. Ever."

"I don't get it," Lisa said, not getting it. Men were like play toys to her. If she saw one she wanted, she went after him. No question about it. The fact that Father Tom was, well, a father, was of no consequence. She gave a heavy sigh, holding her mug of coffee. "Eff my life. I'm so lonely."

"Mommy, Aunt Lisa said 'Eff,'" Matilda declared, scandalized.

"I know. She'll be writing a check for the swear jar before she leaves."

"Swear Jar? You've got to be fucking kidding me," Lisa said in her usual direct manner.

Matilda's eyes were now full saucers; Javier shot daggers but remained silent, probably afraid to open his mouth and risk the Dragon's wrath. He gave me a warning look instead.

"A *really* big check," I said to Matilda. "She'll be underwriting our next trip to Disneyland."

Matilda was smiling now.

"Sorry. It's the whole not being used to kids thing," my obnoxious, single, childless friend said to my daughter, leaning over to her in her seat. "When I'm a mommy, I'll stop using bad words, I promise."

Javier's snort startled me; Lisa scowled, and I watched as Matilda got out of her chair and walked over to the counter where the canisters were lined up beneath the windowsill. She stood on tiptoe and reached for the glass canning jar, the one which held a few stray quarters and dimes inside, shaking it in front of Lisa's face like a holiday bell-ringer.

"Maybe I'll try the goldfish," Lisa said, looking straight at me, deadpan.

"Poor goldfish," Javier said. Lisa stuck her tongue out at him.

"Will you take an IOU?" she asked my eager daughter.

"I'll cover it. This time," I said.

The good thing was that Matilda hadn't yet mastered the art of adding currency; they hadn't gone over coin denominations in kindergarten, so her skill set was limited to knowing quarters were worth the most, but dimes, nickels, and pennies were often intermixed. I found my coin purse and dropped two quarters in the jar. She grinned, happy.

"You know, the other day, I came across something interesting on the news," Javier said. Lisa remained in her slumped position, nursing a second cup of coffee. I feigned interest since I was already on thin ice with my spouse.

"Oh really, dear? What was that?"

Javier cleared his throat and stared pointedly at Lisa. "In Mexico, there is a town called Juchitan that is run completely by women. They're in charge of the businesses—economics, finance, everything. The men work on the farms, give them children, the women take care of the rest."

My friend, who had been slumped over, was now in a fully upright and locked position. He had her attention.

"*That* is where I need to be. You must tell me everything about this fantasy utopia," she said to Javier, in all seriousness.

I gave him a funny look.

"What?" he asked, all lamby-foo-foo innocence.

I shook my head. "Nothing." Clearly Lisa packing up and heading for a remote Mexican village would be a dream come true for him. Still, she was my oldest, dearest friend, and I'd miss her.

"There's only one problem," Lisa said, depressed. "I don't speak Spanish."

"Berlitz, baby," Javier said. A smile had taken up his entire face. I felt my devil horns coming out and couldn't help adding, "What about Frank? He can teach you. I'm sure he'd be *more* than happy to."

Lisa's face clouded over. "Well, probably not Frank. I mean, I really don't want to bother him."

Javier, unaware of Lisa's prior interaction with his father and some sort of bondage scenario, went on describing the merits of the magical-sounding alpha woman's paradise.

"…and the women hold the purse strings. *And* they decide how many children, if any, they'll have. The men simply exist to serve them."

Lisa was practically drooling. I wasn't worried. But it was her life. If she really wanted to drop everything and run away to a remote Mexican village, that was entirely her option.

One thing I knew: my friends were beginning to give me a headache. And it wasn't from the alcohol. Well, maybe some of it was from the alcohol. Mostly, though, it was them.

By midafternoon, after sending Sylvia home hung over, I pruned my yellow rose bush in the area of planter located between our house and Doris's. Pruning is something I do when I need to think and want to get some sun. My friends were gone; the sun was out. I took advantage of the half-hour break during which time Javier and Matilda had gone to the market. I snipped the dead rose hips, saving them for Ofelia's tea, one of her many home remedies. She tells me the rose clippings are full of vitamin C and other things.

The older woman made her way across the street when she saw me, joining me for a chat as she did every now and then when the opportunity arose.

"Are those for me?" she asked, eyeing the little pile I'd put off to the side on the grass.

"All yours. How's Sylvia feeling?"

The older woman's eyebrows were knitted with worry. "She's not well. I worry about her. She's not herself lately."

This was true. Sylvia was going through changes, kind of like puberty, but twenty-two years later.

"Oh, I wouldn't worry about her," I said, doing my best to sound reassuring.

"I do though, Julia. I do."

Poor Ofelia. She stood before me, apron tied around her waist, a dish towel draped across her shoulder, the picture of a long-serving wife and mother if there ever was one. She held her weathered chin with one hand and sighed. I knew that look. I'd seen it plenty of times before—the worried mother look. I'd caused my own dear mother to have that look a time or two hundred. One day Matilda would be putting me through the same type of agony. I mean, if there really were such a thing as justice in the universe.

"Is there something troubling you?"

The old woman shook her head and looked at the sky for a moment.

"The pink behind the clouds is pretty, don't you think?"

It was a quarter to five; the winter sun was beginning to set. It felt like Sylvia's mother had more on her mind than the sunset though.

I tried again. "Ofelia, is everything okay?"

Some people have a hard time sharing their feelings with others; I have to remind myself of this every once in a while. Not everyone believes in sharing every detail about themselves. Some people actually believe in something called "privacy." Oh, and "boundaries."

The older woman sighed. "It's just, I guess I'm disappointed."

"Oh?"

"Don't take this the wrong way, like I'm blaming you or anything," she said with her hand out in front of her as if she were trying to assure me of something.

"Okay, I promise. I won't."

"It's just—" She scratched the top of her head, pausing. I waited, giving her time. She sighed again and continued, "I was *really* hoping things would work out with Sylvia and Ignacio last night," she said, sighing a deep sigh of lost hopes, and dreams gone away in a poof.

And there it was. Ofelia was having the same feelings I'd experienced so many times before—feelings of abject failure and self-loathing as a result of a fix-up gone wrong. Or something like that. But in this case, the person being fixed up wasn't a friend, or even a brother. It was her daughter. This was the big time; I'm talking the realm of future grandchildren and a daughter's happiness. It was heavy stuff.

"Oh," I repeated, for once feeling at a loss for words.

"*Mija*, it's okay. Don't feel bad. I didn't want that; I've just waited all these years for my daughter to find a man. And, you know, she never has." She threw her hands up in the air, then closed her eyes and crossed herself. I think she was praying—probably something resembling the prayer she said whilst making Sylvia's lunch each day.

I so wanted to make things right—everything in poor Ofelia's world. It was a quest. No, it was beyond a quest; it was a mission. Or are those two the very same things?

Whether it would be a quest or a mission, or both, I found myself more determined than ever to find a man for Sylvia.

Chapter Twenty-One

Ted wrestled with the automated single-serve coffee machine, the kind where a person almost has to have a PhD in coffee science to operate. Roger, my boss and owner of Acme Medical Supply Company, had the idea of taking the hassle out of coffee preparation—and it may have had something to do with the fact that neither one of us was capable of making a decent pot—so he bought this crazy-expensive coffee system where a person can select anything from tea to hot cocoa to all manner of coffee-related drinks. The flaw in Roger's plan was that his coffee system turned out to be much more of a hassle than your run-of-the mill Mr. Coffee, causing me to, more often than not, run next door to the Coffee Bean, Tea & Leaf.

"Do you need a hand?" I offered as he smacked the machine twice with the palm of his hand. I'd never seen him looking so obviously vexed; it was very out of character for him.

"Everything okay?"

He ran a hand through his uncharacteristically messy hair.

"Rough weekend?"

He nodded, disgusted. "I'm in serious need of coffee at this point."

"Well, the problem is, you need to be smarter than the machine," I said, joking with him. No reaction. Not the barest hint of a smile. He didn't seem to appreciate my attempt at levity. "Um, sorry?" I apologized. "Want to go next door; we can maybe talk about what's bothering you?"

"I'll get my coat."

Ted seemed to have a serious case of the blues. I got my fleece-lined jacket—the one I saved for the coldest LA days, the days when the temperature actually hovers in the low fifties—and we left the office. In the elevator down, Ted apologized.

"I'm sorry. It's just that I had a disappointing weekend," he said, his tone unhappy.

I put my hand up to my forehead, pretending to be a psychic. "I see your mother involved somewhere in this." He nodded. "Wait. I'm getting something else. It's a woman."

Ted put his forefinger up to his nose, patting it twice, as if we were playing charades.

"Bingo."

"Wait," I said as the elevator came to a stop, "don't tell me anything else until we're sitting down. I want to give you my undivided attention."

We walked to the coffee place next door, getting in the small midmorning line behind a group of women from one of the nearby offices. When it was our turn, I ordered our mochas. The mocha cappuccino I consider to be the ultimate drink, mixing two things I hold dear: chocolate *and* coffee.

This time, he found an open table in the busy coffeehouse as I picked up our order.

"Okay," I said as I handed him his drink, "tell me all about it. Every last little detail, including the little things you think might be insignificant or unimportant."

He smiled, clearly humoring me. I was intrigued, no doubt about it, and waited anxiously to hear details of his ill-fated matchup. There's nothing a matchmaker enjoys more than hearing other matchmaking tales, especially failed arrangements, the whole schadenfreude thing.

He took a deep breath and plunged in. "Well, you know my mother's crazy."

"I'm totally aware of that." The woman was completely off her rocker. "Continue."

"She's been trying to set me up with this girl Sandra for months now."

I nodded; it was just as I thought. His expression was pained. "And?" I said, gesturing with my hand for him to go on.

"So I finally gave in, went to her parents' house for dinner, but I didn't want to."

"And?" I was getting frustrated with Ted who seemed reluctant to give me the whole story. He sighed. I sighed. "What happened?"

"I blew it. I didn't take it seriously, I wore bad clothes, didn't spend time on my appearance so I could look my best. My hair was a *mess*."

I tried not to smile, but it was funny, listening to Ted open up to me about such typical girl-talk things as outfits and hair. Ted was turning out to be a bona fide metrosexual, something I'd always suspected, especially knowing how he coordinated his socks so carefully with his different outfits, and how his ties were expensive silks.

He continued, outlining for me exactly how he went wrong. "I went in with a bad attitude, which totally threw me off when she turned out to be someone really nice. I mean, someone I could see myself asking out." He took a sip of his mocha and set it down, distractedly playing with the stirrer, tapping it on the side of the cup.

The feelings I experienced were contradictory: sadness for poor lonely, wretched Ted, with no one to share his bed except his neurotic bachelor cat, but also relief that things didn't work out with this nice girl and that he was still free for Sylvia. Then I felt immediately guilt for being such a horrible person. Luckily, the angel of my better nature took over; I attempted to give guidance to my poor lovelorn friend.

"Ted," I said clearly and directly, staring into his handsome green eyes with the long, dark lashes. "Call her."

"But—"

"No buts," I said, shutting him down immediately. "No. Call her. Ask her out on a date. What have you got to lose?"

"What if she thinks I'm a big douche?"

I shouldn't have taken a drink right then. I choked on my mocha, gasping, "*What* did you say?"

"I'm serious. I was a jerk."

After my coughing spell, I scolded him. And he couldn't have been *that* bad. It was inconceivable.

"So she thinks you're a douche—which you're very much *not* —and she doesn't go out with you. So what?"

"Then I guess I spend the rest of my life alone with my cat."

How sad. The line from a Beatles song about lonely people flickered through my head. The violins played softly, sadly, in the background of Eleanor Rigby's cemetery. Why *were* there so many lonely people in the world? With seven billion people on the planet, how was it possible people could still find themselves alone?

Yet Ted was. So I dug deep inside myself, accessing the really self-less part of me, the one that I don't access too often.

"Ted, I have an idea."

"Uh-oh," he teased me with eyebrows raised.

"Listen, do you want me to help you, or not?"

"I'm listening," he said with a little smile. He'd perked up ever so slightly.

Sitting across from Ted, I'd had a bit of a brainstorm. Javier had been working like crazy the past month putting finishing touches on his paintings. There was an opportunity on the horizon for a matchup, just *not* the matchup I'd been hoping for.

"Well, Javier's going to be showing some of his paintings at his friend's gallery. The show opens in a couple of weeks. You could invite her to the reception. It'll be very neat, very classy—glasses of wine and bite-size pieces of cheese with those toothpicks that have the little cellophane tips. You could bring her. I could be a buffer."

"Buffer?"

"You know, I could keep the conversation going, the drinks flowing. Make her laugh; tell her what a great guy you are. You know, lie," I said with a little wink.

He laughed and ran a hand through his messy hair, thinking it over. I'd cheered him up, given him a new goal. But at the same time, I had the feeling that he was slipping away from me, out of Sylvia's grasp.

But what else could I do?

Chapter Twenty-Two

Javier's paintings, five in all, were grouped together on one wall of his friend Jose's art gallery. Javier paints religious-themed iconography with a twist; his art depicts the typical icons but puts them in incongruous settings. My favorite of his group depicted the Virgin of Guadalupe with outstretched arms; her billowy robe had become a cape, her clothing a uniform of blue-and-gold tights. She soared through the clouds, over the Hill of Tepeyac, with a determined look in her eyes as if she were on a mission to save the human race. The Blessed Virgin had become Wonder Woman.

"I love this one, babe," I said to Javier, who'd walked up and put his arm around my waist. "I'm going to hate to see it go."

"Well, we might be taking it home with us," he said, his voice tinged with anxiety.

It was typical. Javier always fears the worst with his paintings, but they sell. This one was marked the highest; Jose was asking thirty-eight hundred for it.

Javier leaned in, whispering into my ear, "You look beautiful tonight."

He still had a way of making me feel ten years younger; I felt myself swoon a little. It had been so long since I'd gotten myself really decked out. Having a child has a tendency of putting the reins on evenings out. I wore my little black cocktail dress and heels, simple diamond stud earrings, nighttime makeup. I looked hot. So did Javier in his black jacket and silk T-shirt. It was a real grown-up evening.

We waited for the guests to arrive. The wait staff handed us glasses of mineral water and tapas. I was practically bursting with pride and had to stop myself from eating a whole plate of teeny-tiny slices of Spanish ham paired with hunks of brie and cheddar. The garlic shrimp was sonnet worthy.

"Slow down there, babe. There's more," Javier said as I stuffed food into my mouth. When he's nervous, he doesn't eat; when I'm nervous, I nibble like crazy. Not that there was anything to be nervous about; it was more anticipatory nibbling and not wanting to drink wine on an empty stomach, get tipsy, and say something that would embarrass him.

"How are you holding up?" I asked him. He'd been pacing the gallery, walking in circles, hovering here and there, talking with the other artists, almost constantly on the move, like a nervous jungle cat.

"Don't mind me," he said, rubbing his temples. "I think I'm just going to hide in the back for a couple of hours. Come and get me when it's over."

Poor guy. I motioned for the handsome young waiter with the glasses of sangria, taking two from his tray.

"Here," I said, holding them out to him. Javier took one and gave it a distracted glance. "Drink," I instructed.

He shook his head and handed the glass back to me, leaving me with my hands full. I had no choice but to drink them both, which had the effect of making me much less nervous, and slightly drunk.

By eight, the gallery was full. I watched from my perch atop a stool near Javier's grouping of paintings. Jose, the gallery's owner, had given me business card duty. I was to hand each patron one of the cards after first schmoozing them up, complimenting them and making them feel welcomed. I eavesdropped as an interesting couple next to me—a man with a foot-high Mohawk and a woman wearing a rhinestone-studded turquoise jumpsuit paired with glittery silver platform shoes—chatted about Javier's Blessed Virgin/Wonder Woman piece.

"This is a metaphor, I think, for our modern society's lack of spirituality; she's mourning the soullessness, the alienation that exists within us all," the Mohawked gentleman said to his female companion who nodded, uttering a simple, "That's *so* interesting. Insightful."

It was bullshit. I love hearing people postulate what Javier was thinking when he created one of his works of art. Against my better judgment, I couldn't help it, I added my two cents.

"Actually, the artist just really thinks the Blessed Virgin is supercool."

Mohawk Man scowled, and they moved on to the next set of paintings, a series of still lifes painted by an older artist who liked to work with charcoal. I couldn't wait to hear how they'd interpret *her* work. They weren't planning to buy anything anyway, I could tell. They were poseurs who'd dropped in for the free food and entertainment. You could always spot the deep-pocketed art enthusiasts, and these two definitely weren't it.

My father-in-law, looking dashing in his black leather jacket and slicked-back hair sans bandanna but pulled into a neat ponytail, made his way through the crowd. The gallery was so full by this point, the wait staff was now having to make their way through the people by holding their trays overhead.

Frank gave me a kiss on the cheek; I smelled his cologne.

"Old Spice tonight?"

"Hey, it's popular again," he said with a laugh. "Besides, it makes me smell manly."

"Well, it *does* do that."

Frank leaned in close, and said loudly to be heard over the crowd, "How's he doing so far?"

"He's sold four out of five already."

Frank beamed and gave my hand a squeeze. "We've come a long way," he said simply. He didn't need to say any more, the look on his face spoke volumes. He was a proud father, and rightfully so.

"Well done, Dad," I said, patting him on the back. We basked in the glow of our collective warmth for several seconds, standing next to each other before Javier's wall of icons.

"Look who's here with a date," Frank said with eyebrows raised. I followed his eyebrows over to the gallery entrance. It was Ted, who I'd completely forgotten. Shoot.

"Oh, no. I forgot all about poor Ted," I said, smacking myself in the forehead.

He was a deer in headlights, out of his element. But it wasn't the art gallery and the offbeat crowd that had him so discombobulated, it was the woman standing next to him, her mere existence being the sole reason for his discomfiture. I waved, trying to get his attention, but a crowd of people stood between us in the now-packed gallery. He didn't see me.

The young woman was pretty, in a wholesome Doris Day circa nineteen fifty-eight kind of way. She wore a simple A-line blue dress with a strand of pearls. Her blonde hair was cut in a chin-length bob and bangs. The pillbox hat was a surprise, but her outfit, which seemed ironic, fit right in with the rest of the gallery crowd's funky mix of costumes and eclecticism. If I had searched my whole life, I couldn't have found a more perfect match for preppie Ted. It was a happy-sad moment for me. Bittersweet, I guess. Happy for him, sad for Sylvia. And me.

He looked our way; I waved again until he spotted me, making his way through the crowd and introducing me to his date.

"Uh, Julia, I'd like, uh, to introduce you to…"

I leaned in close. Expectant. Waited two seconds. I leaned in closer. Nothing.

"Hi, Ted," I said, giving him a peck on the cheek. "Hello," I said to the woman next to him, offering my hand.

"Hello," she said in a friendly way, not offering her name.

"Uh, this is…uh…"

I wanted to shake him. *Come on. Spit it out, Ted!* The Doris Day look-alike turned her head, studying him. Waiting. I wasn't sure if she was being nice, patiently waiting for him to get his bearings, or if she was simply cruel. He'd, of course, forgotten her name. I leaned in close toward her. "I love your outfit. Has anyone ever told you, you look just like Doris Day?"

"Oh, really? Who's that?"

She was serious. Her blank expression was real. Apparently she'd never watched any old Rock Hudson/Doris Day screwball comedies. I hate it when people don't get obvious pop culture references, as if they grew up in isolation, or worse, without a television. Ted was breathing hard now. His face was red, his brow beaded with perspiration, and he was on the verge of a full-blown panic attack. *Come on, Ted.* I was urging him with my eyes. Nothing.

It was one of those moments where time slows down and the awkwardness is only accentuated, each moment being supremely painful. I wanted to help him, so in my desperation, I did the only thing I could think of: I pretended to lose my balance, bumping into Doris Day, spilling my drink on her, tagging her left breast. I'd been aiming for her shoulder but failed.

I closed my eyes for a split second and opened them to see the look of horror on her face.

"Oh, no. I'm so sorry."

"My dress!" She looked down at her chest and back at me, more shocked than anything.

"Come with me. There's a kitchen in the back. Let's get you cleaned up," I was yelling in her ear over the noise. Ted had darted off, escaping the situation, mumbling something about finding a napkin.

His date, whose name I still hadn't gotten, followed me into the gallery kitchen where we dodged wait staff and gallery patrons. I grabbed a paper towel and a bottle of club soda from the row of bottles sitting on the counter, soaking the paper towel with a little club soda.

"So sorry. I'm so clumsy." I gave her a weak smile, turning on my charm.

"Ugh. It's okay. You didn't mean to."

"Here. Take this," I said, handing her the paper towel. "Dab, don't wipe."

She dabbed the circle-shaped stain. Unfortunately, her dabbing only served to turn the small circle into a larger circle, which gave her the look of a breastfeeding mother whose milk had come in.

"I'm Sandra, by the way."

Finally. I smacked myself in the head. Ted had mentioned her name over coffee. If only I'd remembered it.

"It's so nice to meet you," I said, pumping her hand that wasn't holding the soggy paper towel enthusiastically. "Sorry we had to meet like this."

"Oh, well. Accidents happen," she said, shrugging it off. "It's only vintage." She dabbed and added, "Dior," to rub salt in the wound.

Ouch.

"So, how do you know Ted?" she asked in her detached way.

"We work together." I handed her a dry kitchen towel. "Want to give this a try?"

"I don't think that'll help. It's silk."

Again, ouch.

"Ted's a great guy, isn't he? He's just a godsend at the office. I don't know what we'd do without him."

By her flat expression, I gathered that Sandra was skeptical about Ted and his positive attributes. I tried to pump her up a little about him, get her to see him as the great guy that he truly was and get her excited about her date, which, up to this point, had been a big fat dud.

"Um, he's a nice guy…" she said, agreeing with me. She trailed off, and I felt like there was a "but" there. I waited for the "but." Her eyes darted around the kitchen, stopping when she found the handsome waiter who was taking several bottles of champagne out of the refrigerator. "He's kind of a mess though." She shook her head. "So awkward. I can't get him to look me in the eye."

She was staring at the waiter now, following him with her eyes as he walked by, carrying his tray of half-filled champagne glasses. She smiled at him; he smiled back. He was good-looking. I was kind of getting an idea about her taste—muscular, dark, and handsome. Not Ted, who was handsome, but not the dark and muscular part. Ted was not a guy who exuded manliness. My protective instincts were beginning to take over; I gave it another shot.

"Oh, he's maybe a little shy. He's so handsome though, don't you think? And he's really fun."

Her nose wrinkled when I said "fun." I felt like a used car salesman. I wanted her to like him. Really like him.

"He's not my type," she tossed off dismissively.

"Um, so why are you here?" I asked pointedly, bordering on rude.

"My parents. Well, my mother. You know how mothers can be."

"Yours too, huh?"

She nodded. "My mother has been nagging me to go out with him for months. I did it so she'd back off," she said with a shrug.

It sounded like her mother and Ted's mother went to the same overbearing mother school. Suddenly, I felt a wave of gratitude for my New Age-hippie-peace-and-love-Birkenstocks-wearing-liberal-vegan mother who never made me do anything or date anyone I didn't want to.

Thank you, Mom, for not sucking.

This girl did not *deserve* Ted. But Sylvia did. I gave myself a pat on the back for doing the right thing. I hadn't sabotaged his date with Sandra. I mean, besides spilling my drink on her. In retrospect, though, she totally deserved it. He'd still have his chance with my friend. My match could *still* possibly work out. I felt a little burst of optimism knowing Ted was safe.

"We should get back to—"

I was about to suggest returning to the others when Frank interrupted.

"Everything okay, ladies?"

Frank. He'd come back to check on us. He was looking concerned and handsome. Frank is very good at faking being concerned.

My devil horns began to emerge, imagining the interesting possibilities.

"Frank, you didn't get a chance to meet Sandra. She's a friend of Ted's."

Predictably, Frank, ever the ladies' man, swooped down on Modern Doris Day, picking up her hand and bringing it to his lips, barely brushing them against her skin.

"It is a pleasure to meet you," he said in his most sexy, low voice. I tried to keep from obviously showing my disdain, quelling my gag reflex.

"Oh, it's so nice to meet you," she said, batting her eyelashes. "Are you Julia's brother-in-law?" she asked, all innocence, pretending to confuse Frank as Javier's brother. She was a smooth operator, like Frank. I wanted to barf, but Frank was all smiles, delighted.

"I'm his father."

"Oh, you must have been a *young* dad," she said and giggled some more.

"Excuse me, you guys, I've got to get back out there."

I took the opportunity to leave them to their flirting. They were already so engrossed in each other's company, they didn't even hear me. Ignored, I went back out to find poor Ted, who was going to go home alone; that much was certain.

I found Ted outside in the cold, standing in front of the gallery. His cheeks and nose were red. It was freezing.

"What *happened* to you in there?" I scolded, wanting to smack him upside the head. For God's sake, here he was, a grown man, completely tongue-tied and useless. Thirty-two years old. "What in the world happened?"

Poor Ted. His eyes were downcast. He was such a little boy. I instantly felt bad for scolding him and instead wanted to fix him a bowl of oatmeal and kiss his boo-boos.

He shook his head, frowned. "I don't know. It's my stupid social phobia."

"You don't have a social phobia. Stop it right now. That's ridiculous."

I was shivering, bouncing in place.

"Here," he said, handing me his sport coat.

"Thanks."

He shook his head. "No, I do. When it comes to women, I lose the ability to speak or at least say something remotely coherent. Forget sounding intelligent or interesting. It's no use." He sighed a sigh of depression and resignation. "I'm such an idiot."

"No, you're not, you're just special."

His eyebrows were raised. "Special?" I'm not sure what made me choose that particular word. But I didn't mean it in the sense that he rode the short bus; I meant that he possessed uncommon, rare qualities in a world of flash and crassness. He was almost a man from a different time—a time when people were more polite, less sucky. I gave it another shot.

"Ted, you are one of the most unique people I've ever met. You're not like every other guy out there, and that *does* make you special. But in the best possible sense of the word. You're like something rare and wonderful."

He stroked his chin with his hand thoughtfully. "Maybe if I'd had a drink beforehand to settle my nerves."

I made a mental note to give him a drink or two before introducing him to Sylvia.

"It's okay," I said softly, comforting him with my arm around his shoulder, giving him a little pat. "Let's get you a glass of wine, then I'm going to have you talk to at least two strange women before you leave. Okay?"

I had become Ted's dating coach; someone had to.

"Could we make it two *not* strange women?" he said with his little smile.

There was hope. A tiny sliver.

"Let's get warm," I said.

We rejoined the party. We mingled and mixed. I found an unattended serving tray that held a few rows of cream cheese and olive finger sandwiches. I offered the plate to Ted; he declined. I stuffed three in my mouth while scanning for practice women. The gallery crowd had thinned out a little, and I spotted a couple of attractive twenty-somethings standing in front of Javier's painting of the Blessed Virgin as Wonder Woman. I signaled with my hand, subtly pointing in their direction, giving Ted the signal to follow my lead. He looked like a man about to receive a prostate exam. "Shrug it off, Ted," I whispered in his ear with authority. We advanced.

"Do you like it?" I asked the tall brunette who wore a gray cloche hat and matching gray wool suit. Her outfit could have been taken straight from a nineteen thirties Agatha Christie novel, but she'd managed to pull off the look.

"It's wonderful. I'm so sad that it's been sold," she said with a frown.

"The artist is my husband."

Her companion, another brunette with a serious face and brooding eyes, chimed in. "He must be *very* good with his hands." The two laughed at her joke.

Like I've never heard *that* line before.

"Is *he* your husband?" the woman wearing the cloche hat asked. She was referring to Ted, who was pretending to show interest in a nearby painting which, unfortunately, was of a very large phallus. I'm convinced the artist had some serious daddy issues she was working through at the time. Either that or she really liked phalluses.

"Oh, no. He's a friend of mine. Let me get him." It was perfect. I grabbed Ted by the arm, pulling him over. "This is my friend Ted."

Cloche Hat looked him over, up and down, holding her drink casually in her hand, before asking, "Are *you* an artist?"

Ted was flustered, as usual. "Um, no. But I like art."

"You *like* art?"

She glanced at her friend, and the two laughed a laugh of the mean-spirited. I wanted to smack them both upside their pointy heads for their art snobbery. They probably didn't know a Frida Kahlo from a Diego Rivera, but as Ted's wing woman, I had to show some kind of restraint, so I extricated him instead of clunking them over the head with my fist.

"Look, Ted, there are some *much* more interesting people over there," I said with extra enthusiasm.

Cloche Hat and friend gave me a dirty look. We took our leave.

In the world of love, there is no room for cruelty. One thing, however, was clear: I either needed to get him drunker, or find nicer, more approachable women for him to talk to, and the gallery crowd of hipsters, poseurs, and art snobs did *not* show much promise there.

At the end of the night, Javier's show was a great success—for Javier, not Ted. As it turned out, his date Sandra didn't go home with Frank after all. She didn't go home with Ted either. At a quarter of nine, Javier spotted her leaving with the handsome young waiter, so it was a success for her as well.

I went back to my scheming.

Chapter
Twenty-Three

Frank cleaned the enormous birdcage that housed his African gray parrot Esmeralda who sat perched on his shoulder, squawking so loud, my eardrums felt like they were about to split open.

"Settle down, *mi amor*," he said in a soothing voice, trying to get her to calm down, but she was having none of it, squawking and cackling in her ridiculous parroty way.

Something I've learned about parrots from my interactions with Esmeralda over the years is that once they've decided to be talkative, there's nothing to be done—no persuasion or coercion —that will quiet them down.

"*Hola*," the bird squawked in her funny strident voice, bobbing her head.

"*Hola*, Esmeralda," Matilda said upon entering her grandfather's house, and repeated, "*Hola. Hola*," giggling. It never got old.

The energized bird began to bounce up and down on Frank's shoulder. "*Buenos dias*," she squawked. Matilda laughed.

"It's '*buenos noches*,'" Javier corrected.

Frank gave a little shrug. "She's never been good with time."

Javier, carrying the pot of cocido he'd prepared for our Sunday dinner with Frank, inquired, "Pop, where do you want this?"

"Ah, I wasn't expecting you guys so early," my father-in-law said as he tried to take the seed and water cups out of the cage with Esmeralda squawking incessantly in his ear.

"It's six-fifteen," Javier yelled over the bird's cacophony.

"Just put it on the stove, *mijo*. I'll be done here in a minute."

Frank was trying to gain control of the situation. He tried to brush Esmeralda off his shoulder and coax her onto one of the large perches that made up the little branches of a massive freestanding perch shaped in the form of a tree next to her cage. The minute her little bird feet touched one of the tree's branches, she'd hop off, fluttering over to Frank's shoulder again. And again. He sighed, grumbling, "This bird is a pest."

It was funny. I always enjoyed watching the two of them. Matilda got a huge thrill out of this talking animal. But then, who wouldn't?

Matilda hovered next to Frank, watching him clean the cage, repeating in her singsong voice, "*Hola. Hola. Hola,*" and giggling each time the parrot squawked, "*hola,*" back to her.

Poor Frank. He was caught in the middle of his noisy bird and his noisy granddaughter.

"*Mija*, grab the cup in the bottom there, would you?" he said patiently.

She reached her little hands into the cage and pulled out the blue ceramic cup Frank used for cut-up fruit and other things besides seed. "Come with me," he said, and the two disappeared into the kitchen to clean the containers. I listened as Frank tried to make conversation with his granddaughter above the parroty racket—the operative word being "tried."

Javier returned from the kitchen, shaking his head. "Esme's a little loud today."

"I've never seen an animal so attached to its owner," I said. It was quite remarkable.

"She's the most faithful woman in his life," Javier said as we sat down on Frank's worn-out bachelor's couch with the nibbled-on edges. Over the years, Esmeralda had made her presence known throughout the house. Anything made of wood was fair game with scarred edges. Esme was a notorious nibbler.

Javier reached for the television remote to find the football game. What he said about the relationship between Frank and his bird was true. Javier and his little brother Rudy had grown up with the parrot that was like their crazy aunt. She and Frank had been a couple for the past thirty or so years. He'd brought her home one day, shortly after his wife Pam took off. Javier was eight when his mother left with another man. The boys were brokenhearted, and Frank was determined to help them heal their wounds. He fell in love with the kooky bird and her outsize personality. And they *were* like an actual couple, the way she squawked and he argued with her. It was sweet, and poignant.

If only he could find someone to be as constant in *human* form.

"Your dad needs a woman," I said, in a wistful way. "He needs more than his parrot wife. He needs a flesh-and-blood partner."

"No."

"What?" I was wounded by his one-word response.

"Don't even start," Javier said, his eyes glued on the game.

"Why *doesn't* he have a girlfriend?" I asked my husband, expecting an answer to something unanswerable. "Why *didn't* he ever remarry?" Another unanswerable question. It was really more rhetorical, but I was curious to hear Javier's opinion on the subject.

Javier sighed and muted the television. "I don't know. Maybe my mom took it out of him. Or maybe he's never been able to figure out how to pick the right person." He gave a little shrug and turned to look at me. "Or maybe he just didn't get lucky, like I did."

Just when I think I'm aggravated with my husband, he goes and says something so sweet and wonderful, I want to wrap my arms around him and squeeze him.

"Oh, babe. I think I'll keep you." I kissed the side of his face; his eyes were glued back on the game. "I'm going to have to work on finding someone for your dad," I added softly.

Javier, absorbed in the game, grunted, "Mm-hmm."

So it was settled. Frank was on my list. I mean, Javier had given me permission and everything. The question was: whom?

My Lonely Hearts Club list was becoming full, and complicated. Not only were Sylvia and Ted on my to-be-matched list, there was also Lisa, my brother Chris, and now Frank. The hamster wheel in my brain was turning nonstop, but at least both hamsters were running in the same direction this time.

Since it was clear I had my work cut out for me now that I'd taken Frank on, I took the opportunity to help him in the kitchen after dinner. Javier was safely out of earshot in the living room watching the game while Matilda played with Esmeralda.

As Frank loaded the dishwasher, I wiped down his countertops, studying him. I had to keep it casual; I didn't want to arouse his suspicions. I arranged the words carefully in my head, wiping the counter as I said them.

"Frank, you know, you'd look so handsome with a haircut."

He stopped in his tracks, dinner plate in hand.

"What? Where is this coming from? You love my hair."

Shoot. Frank seemed hurt, and that wasn't my intent at all.

"Oh, I do. But I think you'd look even better with some trimming up. Let's call it updating. Get rid of the long, gray hair, have a nice, clean shave—and the 'stache. It's a little *Magnum, P.I.*, isn't it?" I gave him a critical once-over; I couldn't help myself. I was now in full make-over-Frank mode.

"You're up to something, aren't you, *mija?*" he asked suspiciously before recommencing his loading duties. I backed off.

"No, no," I said with a wave of the hand. "Not at all. Jeez, Frank, this soup is all over the range top. What the heck did you do?"

I wiped the stove, trying to change the subject. Silence enveloped the kitchen. But then, as so often happens when you plant a little seed, after a short time, it begins to germinate. As Frank put dishes away and I worked on scrubbing his stove, I watched out of the corner of my eye as he stroked his beard and felt the ends of his outdated handlebars. I could tell, I'd gotten to him. And I wasn't entirely proud of that fact, but sometimes you have to employ harsh tactics when it comes to creating a love match.

Yeah, I'll keep telling myself that.

Chapter Twenty-Four

I met Mickey Martin when I was in the second grade. He was shorter than I was, had shaggy, blond hair, and a great smile. When Lisa told me he liked me, I was immediately smitten. I remember it like it was yesterday.

Lisa came over to my house after school; I'd been home that day with a sprained ankle and crutches. I hobbled to the front door.

In second grade, Lisa was pretty much the way she is today —long, red hair, tall, forceful demeanor, beautiful face, but people gave her space.

"Where were you?" she demanded, hands on her hips.

"Look at my foot."

She looked at my foot. "Does it hurt?"

"Yeah, a lot."

The day before was Sunday, and my brother Chris was riding me up and down the street on the handlebars. The bike's tire caught on a pebble in the road, stopping the bike immediately, but my forward momentum propelled me over the bike's front tire, catching my right foot in the spokes. There I was, lying with my back on the asphalt and my foot caught in his tire, howling in pain as he hovered over me.

"Are you okay?" he asked in a near panic.

"No," I wailed.

A trip to the ER later, and I was sent home with a pair of crutches and diagnosis of a sprain. The ankle had swollen up like a softball.

Lisa followed me as I hobbled into the living room and sat on the couch next to me.

"I have something important to tell you." She looked around, making sure there was no one within earshot. "Mickey Martin likes you."

Mickey Martin. I thought about it for a second or two. He was really cute. Shorter than me by a couple of inches, and fast. He was about the fastest boy in class, probably because he was so small and closer to the ground.

"Well, what do you think?" Lisa's eyes were on me, probing. She's always been a direct person. "Do you like him?"

"Yeah, I do."

"Okay, then. Are you coming to school tomorrow?"

I looked down at my swollen foot. "I don't know."

"That's too bad," she said, disappointed, "because I'm going to tell him you like him."

"Well, won't he still like me the day after tomorrow?"

Her nose wrinkled as she contorted her face, thinking. "I'm not sure. Brenda K. likes him too, so he might switch over to her if you're not there tomorrow."

That was a predicament. I felt my ankle, seeing if it still felt tender and sore.

"I'm gonna soak my foot some more," I said. "Maybe I'll be at school."

She nodded. "Okay. I've gotta go."

Later that afternoon, my mother ran a tub of hot water and filled it with Epsom salts, so I could soak my foot some more. I was determined to be at school the next day and fight for my man —the man I didn't know I loved until almost that very moment.

Somehow, I made it to school the next day, hobbling with my crutches and mostly hopping. My brother Chris, who was in sixth grade at the time, felt completely awful about my injury and carried my book bag for me. I was able to milk his guilt for weeks afterward.

Things worked out between Mickey and me, and for the rest of the school year, he picked me up in the morning and carried my book bag for me as we walked. It was very romantic. After school we'd race each other home. He won every time. Even missing one of his front teeth, he was dreamy. And the way his sandy, blond hair would fall over his eyes when he talked to me was irresistible.

We lost touch the summer after second grade, and in third grade, he'd moved on to Little League, and I'd moved on to Brownies. It's not that we had a fight and broke things off; it was more that we drifted away from each other. But I learned from my experience with Mickey that love, even puppy love, is a wonderful thing.

A picture of Mickey and me is what prompted my trip back in time. I'd been putting things away in the garage during my annual New-Year organization effort, which this year had spilled into mid-February, when I came across my box of elementary school mementos. I found the picture of the two of us that my parents had taken. In it, we were sitting on the front porch steps, his arm around me. I wore a little pink skirt, frilly socks, and a purple sweater. He wore jeans and a Spiderman T-shirt. I was smiling; he had an adorable grin on his face; his bangs were covering one eye. He looked like a puppy dog.

I felt wistful holding the picture in my hand, thinking about being young and innocent before the harsh realities of life had taken their toll. We looked so happy. There was another picture, one showing the two of us and Lisa, standing in my front yard. In this picture, Lisa was wearing a short-short skirt—typical—and had her hand on her hip in a bossy manner. Also typical. It struck me as I looked at the three of us how natural love came to me, yet here Lisa, the one who had brought Mickey and me together, was alone.

Why was this one emotion so elusive for some people? Wasn't love one of the most basic elements of life along with the need for oxygen and food? I looked at the picture and had an epiphany: Lisa, of all people in the world, had played matchmaker for me at least once. Also, it was because of her I'd met Javier. It was time to return the favor.

But I felt like there were serious questions that needed answering, so I did what I always do when faced with one of life's big questions: I called my big brother for advice.

Two hours later, we met at the Denny's near his church. I sat across from him in our booth, studying him. At almost forty, Chris was still boyish-looking. His hair was lightened from the sun, his skin tanned, and his eyes bright blue; the skin crinkling at the corners when he smiled, which was often. He could have passed for a surfer, which he also was, maybe not so much as a priest.

"So what is this all about?" he asked, looking earnest, ready to help as always.

We waited for our salads to arrive; I played with my napkin.

"I need spiritual advice."

He cocked his head to the side slightly. "Okay," was all he said. Apparently, I was to take the lead, so I plunged forward.

"It's maybe not so much spiritual advice as it is existential."

He was watching my face; his expression was calm and even. My brother is a very good listener. He also reads facial cues. One thing about talking to him, I know I have to tell the truth because he's like a human lie detector and can spot any kind of inaccuracies or weaknesses in a story.

"Well—" he paused and cleared his throat "—I've got my thoughts about things, but what exactly did you want to know?" he asked patiently.

I thought for a second and asked him, "Why do some people have such a hard time finding love?"

It was a simple question, but when it came down to it, that was really what I wanted to know. In a world created by God, who knows all things and is in charge, why—if He created it—was the whole thing so damned complicated?

Chris thought for a second. "You know, that's a very good question."

I felt all warm and fuzzy inside, just as if the teacher had given me an A-plus.

"I thought so. I worked really hard on that one."

He smiled. "Well, this may disappoint you, but it's the whole 'free will' concept. He gave us the ability to think for ourselves. Human emotions are much too complex, love being the most complex of all of them. It's not a one-size-fits-all scenario. But, if it helps you, God wants us all to be happy. He wants us all to live in love and walk in love."

I'd suspected I'd get this kind of response from him. Still, it was disappointing. The server brought our salads, but before diving in, I had one more question.

"So if God wants us to have love, then is it wrong for me to try to bring two people together?"

Chris had just taken a bite of Cobb salad; his mouth was full, his eyes wide. I'd caught him off guard with that one. And I'd impressed myself. The question, after his preceding explanation, seemed to dictate an answer that was favorable to my cause. If we believed in a loving God, then how could it be wrong to help two lonely souls find the very thing God wanted for them? I was practically patting myself on the back over this one.

He swallowed first before dabbing his mouth delicately with his napkin and answering. "Nice try."

"What do you mean?"

He was shaking his head, laughing. "I know you. Here I thought you had a legitimate existential crisis. I should've known better."

"Come on, Chris," I protested. By this time, I was in a full-blown pout.

He sighed. "Julia, you've been trying to match people up since you were in diapers."

That was *not* true. At least not that I had any memory of. I pressed him. "How can there be anything wrong with bringing people together?"

He put a hand out and started ticking off reasons with the pointer finger of his other hand: "Let's see. There's awkward feelings. That's one. Dates from hell. There's another. Incompatibility issues…" He was now holding up three fingers with the other two folded over. "I still remember that horrendous evening with Michael." He shuddered. I felt myself dying a little on the inside as he continued on, blissfully unconcerned with the pain he was inflicting. Very mean of a priest, if you ask me. "Julia, we all know you *mean* well, but there's *nothing* worse than being on the wrong end of a bad date. Simple as that. *That* is why you shouldn't get involved in other people's love lives, and I'm *certainly* not giving you permission to do so," he said with finality.

I wouldn't concede his point. No way. Instead, I jumped right in with both feet.

"So," I asked innocently, picking at my salad, "have you met anyone interesting lately?"

He sighed. "No." It was a sore subject, I could tell. "I'm too busy, you know, church stuff. There's always something—someone to visit in the hospital, outreach, people in crisis."

Poor Chris. He was a little depressed now.

"So how does that help the flock when the person in charge of their care is the most miserable?"

"I didn't say I was the *most* miserable," he said, indignant.

"Oh, you know what I mean. It's not fair. You shouldn't have to sacrifice your happiness like that. Isn't there anyone interesting in the congregation? Anyone you see when you look out over the crowd and think, 'I'd like a little piece of that'?"

He practically choked on his herbal tea.

"Julia! What is wrong with you? You *know* I can't date parishioners. It's messy, not to mention wrong. It's a total no-no." He rubbed the side of his face, thinking it over. "Plus, the eligible bachelors are either in their sixties or they're too young."

So he *had* thought of it.

"Look, brother, it's one thing to devote your life to work; it's another to become a martyr for it, sacrificing your own social life. *That* is messed up, and you know it."

"You're right," he said with a nod. "I'm just a big coward."

I felt bad now. He felt exposed; I'd been chastised. Nothing right had come out of our meeting. I didn't get the answers I was looking for, and I felt like stamping my foot and puffing out my lower lip, saying, "It's not fair," like when we were kids. We ate in silence for a few moments, pondering, then Chris, with a fork in one hand, pointing his little bit of hard-boiled egg and lettuce at me, said, "You still shouldn't play God with people's romantic lives."

"Fine. See if I try to set you up with anyone again," I said, defiant.

"There is a God," he said, completely deadpan.

Smartass.

But I had a thought to share, because I refused to go quietly. "Do you mean to tell me the whole ages-old idea of matchmaking has no place in this world?"

He chewed and thought. "No, that's not what I'm saying." He paused and looked me straight in the eyes and said, "It's just that it doesn't work the way *you* do it." He said this softly, trying not to wound me too deeply, although the knife had been plunged deep into my solar plexus. "I'm sorry," he said with some tenderness. "You know I love you more than anything in the world, but you're so…so…" He trailed off. I sat on the edge of the bench waiting for his final pronouncement.

"So…what? What?"

"Spontaneous." He nodded, agreeing with himself. "That's the word I was looking for."

I slumped in my seat, crushed. "What's wrong with being spontaneous? Isn't spontaneity a highly sought-after trait? Spontaneous people, by definition, are fun to be around, quite delightful. Everyone knows this. It's a universal truth."

He laughed. "Yes, you're right. All of that is true. Except when it comes to making a match." He smiled, looking just like a priest, bringing his hands together under his chin, almost clasped in prayer. "There are so many of those lovely little intangibles that go into bringing two people together. You, of all people, should know this. You can't just go flying in and creating a couple where the very issue of compatibility remains unresolved."

He was right. I was *too* spontaneous. For a priest, he really could be the most annoying person in the world. Annoyingly right.

But, now that I knew what to fix, there was hope. More hope than I had when I'd gotten up that morning. Chris's comments were my challenge. Unbeknownst to him, he'd thrown down the gantlet.

And there's nothing I love more than a challenge.

Chapter
Twenty-Five

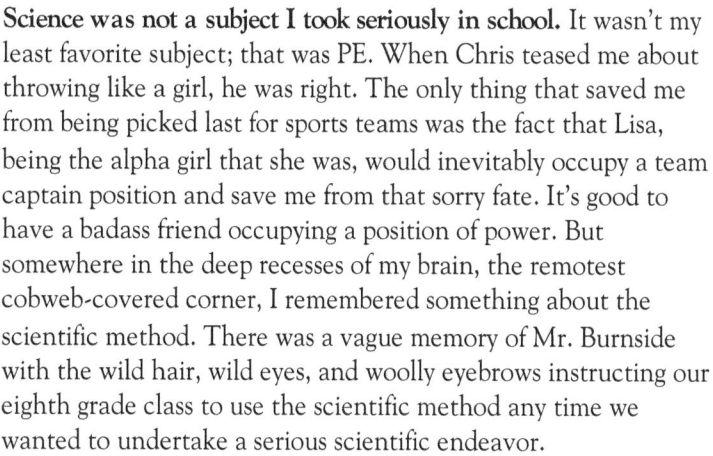

Science was not a subject I took seriously in school. It wasn't my least favorite subject; that was PE. When Chris teased me about throwing like a girl, he was right. The only thing that saved me from being picked last for sports teams was the fact that Lisa, being the alpha girl that she was, would inevitably occupy a team captain position and save me from that sorry fate. It's good to have a badass friend occupying a position of power. But somewhere in the deep recesses of my brain, the remotest cobweb-covered corner, I remembered something about the scientific method. There was a vague memory of Mr. Burnside with the wild hair, wild eyes, and woolly eyebrows instructing our eighth grade class to use the scientific method any time we wanted to undertake a serious scientific endeavor.

The scientific method required taking several steps, starting with the particular question relating to the particular experiment. In my case, my question was: How do I improve on my matchmaking results? This was critical, and since I'd already conceded Chris's point that my spontaneity had been getting me into trouble, I'd made the momentous decision to take my matchmaking to an entirely different level.

With "the question" decided, my next steps would include background research, constructing a hypothesis, testing that hypothesis with an experiment, analyzing the data, drawing a conclusion, and reporting my results. I actually wouldn't render a formal report to anyone, but that was the process, in a nutshell. This was all very technical, but research seemed to be the key to getting me to the next step.

At work, I found an unused clipboard and placed several sheets of paper on the board and clipped them together. While my coworkers worked, while Ted pecked away at his keyboard balancing a ledger, or whatever it was he did all day, I sat at my desk writing. The orders would have to wait. My system was simple; I allotted two pieces of paper per test subject. The subjects of my study were: Ted, Sylvia, Lisa, and Frank.

Because he was closest in proximity—about fifteen feet away from where I sat—Ted was first up. I studied him carefully and made little bullet points for likes, dislikes, pros and cons, pluses and minuses. In a stream of consciousness, I wrote everything I knew about Ted. For instance, Ted liked poetry—especially Proust—preferred cats over dogs, argyle sweaters over windbreakers, half-caf cappuccinos over regular coffee, fine clothes, and steampunk novels. For dislikes, I listed his mother, Thai food, anchovies on pizza, dark beer, lowbrow humor, and reality television.

Every once in a while, I'd ask him a random question.

"Ted, what do you think about women with dark hair? Do you like it?"

He looked up from what he was doing, puzzled. "Um, I guess so. Why do you ask?"

"Oh, I was thinking of dyeing my hair."

"Why would you want to do that?"

"I'm not saying I'll actually *do* it. Just thinking about it."

Twenty minutes later, I asked, "Ted, what's your stance on breast implants?"

"And you're asking this *why*? You look *fine*, Julia. Your clothes hang better with a smaller chest anyway."

Gee, thanks, Ted.

"Me? Oh, no. A friend is."

"Um, well, I'm, uh, not sure I have strong feelings either way."

I wrote down his response: "Lukewarm to fake breasts."

Later: "And how do you feel about religion?"

He had his phone to his ear and waved me off. He finished his call. "Julia, is there something I'm not getting here? Are you taking a survey?"

"Mmm, of sorts. Let's just say I'm compiling information." I held the clipboard, pen in hand. "So, religion? Important? Yes, no?"

"Uh, wow. If I were to best describe my thoughts on religion, I'd identify myself as agnostic. I believe there's probably someone in charge, but I'm not sure. My parents were so—"

"That's fine," I cut him off. Time was of the essence since I had actual work to do, and Roger, my boss, was due back from his golf game any time. For religious preferences, I put none.

By the end of the day, I'd amassed a fair amount of information on Ted. What I was going to do with this information, I wasn't sure. I still had three more profiles to fill in.

Lisa's was easy. We'd been friends so long, there weren't many secrets between us, but if I was going to take this whole scientific method seriously, I had to remain faithful to the format, so the day after I'd taken Ted's inventory, I sat at my desk to work on Lisa's. Under likes, I almost didn't know where to start. Men were a given, but "men" was just the top of the personality pyramid. She liked tall men, but she didn't mind short men. Good-looking wasn't necessarily a given, thinking back on the men she'd dated over the years. I thought of one interesting guy, Sean, who had an uncanny resemblance to a werewolf—thick shaggy eyebrows and a very hairy face. Lisa's type of man ran the gamut. Breathing was a must. Physical endurance was another.

I sat absorbed at my desk, sucking on my pen. Since she seemed to like all sorts of men, I thought it would be easier to write down what she disliked in a man. The section remained blank. It was harder than I thought. *What didn't she like?* I asked myself. Pushy, aggressive behavior. Of course. I smacked myself in the head. She bossed men around for a living. Naturally, she'd prefer a man who'd let her boss him around in real life. Know-it-all types were also out. Overly sensitive wouldn't work either—too much like a woman.

For likes, qualities she would be attracted to in a mate, I wrote "Easygoing." I also wrote "Experimental types who enjoy whips and electric tools." I probably shouldn't have written that down; it looked bad on the page. Lisa also liked sex; that went without saying, but I added it to the list in the interest of completeness. For music: hard rock and heavy metal. Religion: none. Political affiliation: none.

Dislikes: children; cute and fuzzy things—anything bearing a resemblance to a baby animal; movies rated below R; sweet.

Lisa, on paper, when I added up her attributes, kind of sucked. But she was loyal, and tough. And if I ever needed someone to help me out in a knife fight, she'd have my back. And ultimately, I suppose, *that* is what true friendship is all about.

My clipboard was full of information; at least half of it was useful.

Sylvia was next on my list.

As far as men went, her likes seemed to run toward the unobtainable. That was a problem. Since Father Tom was the only one out of her long line of crushes whom I'd had any personal contact with, I needed extra information, which was why I unexpectedly found myself accompanying her to confession.

My life = not boring.

I'd made the mistake of innocently calling her to pump her for information. It was the end of the workday on Friday.

"Sylvia, do you have a few minutes? Can you talk?"

"Oh, Julia. I'm so glad you called. I'm running out the door right now. I could really use your moral support."

Interesting.

"Um, okay. Why?"

"Well, you know how I feel about Father Tom; right?"

"Um, yes, I think I'm familiar with your feelings about Father Tom," I said calmly, while at the same time pretending to hang myself with an imaginary noose.

"I'm going to confess, and I need you—"

"Wait a second," I butted in, "confess to who?"

"It's to whom," she said, correcting my grammar. I knew better; I was rattled by her little pronouncement. "I've been thinking, and I thought if I could just come clean, confess my feelings formally, maybe I'd be able to stop obsessing over him and move on with my life."

It *sounded* reasonable enough, but I seemed to be detecting a note of hysteria in her voice. As it turned out, I was right. She'd apparently worked herself into a state of half despondency, half irrationality. She needed help. My help.

She rattled on, "I've been so upset, so frustrated with myself. I'm not getting anywhere with my life. I'm stuck—"

"Whoa. Slow down," I said, cutting her off. I glanced at the oversize clock on the wall and sighed. "I can leave here in fifteen minutes, be there in half an hour. Does that work?"

"All right. If I get there first, I'll wait for you in the back of the church."

It was a deal. I sighed again, packed my clipboard in my laptop case, and went to meet Sylvia. In a church. For confession. Something I'd never pictured myself doing on a Friday afternoon.

Chapter Twenty-Six

Sylvia was sitting in the very last pew. I shivered; the church was colder inside than it was outside. There were a couple of older women waiting near a wooden confessional that reminded me of an oversize, inlaid-mahogany armoire; otherwise, the church was empty. I sat down next to her; she turned to me with sad eyes.

"Have you gone in yet?" I asked.

"I can't."

"Why not?"

"Father *Tom's* inside," she whispered in despair.

"Can I go with you inside? Is that allowed?"

I thought it was worth a shot. "Confessing" is something I have no experience with, but it seemed like a reasonable thing to do, especially for a friend in turmoil.

She thought for a second, her forehead wrinkled. "I don't think you're supposed to, but I don't think it would hurt."

"Let's do it then," I whispered. "Come on."

It was a tight fit. Sylvia went in first, bunching herself up next to the wall of the wooden booth. We shared the bench, our hips touching. The priest opened the little sliding door/window thingy. It was fascinating, the whole process. Very cool. I made a quick mental rundown of things I could unload on him so I could rid myself of any unresolved guilt and then reminded myself that that wasn't what we were there for. But really, I think I could fill a *lot* of time with the padre.

I waited for Sylvia to say something. She took a deep breath and crossed herself. The priest on the other side of the divider cleared his throat and waited patiently.

Thirty seconds have a way of feeling like forever when you're squeezed into a stuffy wooden box next to a nervous woman about to confess her forbidden love to the priest she's obsessed with.

Again, not my usual Friday afternoon.

Sylvia crossed herself again for double strength, saying, "Bless me, Father, for I have sinned. It's been three months since my last confession."

"Bless you, my child. What's on your mind?"

It was the first time I'd heard Father Tom speak. He had a nice, calm voice. Not necessarily sexy, but comforting, like a big brother. The kind of reassuring voice you'd expect from a priest.

Sylvia closed her eyes, took another deep breath to compose herself, and wrapped her fingers around a lock of hair, twisting it nervously.

"Father, I'm having feelings for someone that I shouldn't." She paused and looked at me. I shrugged my shoulders, gesturing in the air with my hand, urging her to continue.

"This man is, ah, unavailable to me, and I've been struggling with my feelings for him. I want him to be with me, yet he's obligated to...to someone else."

Poor thing. She obviously wanted to die right on the spot. I gave her shoulder a pat in solidarity. Father Tom's voice was soft and soothing as he gave his words of comfort.

"My child, you know this man is not for you. Maybe he's married; maybe he has a wife and family? Whatever his circumstances, you know this, and that's what's important. You have the conscience of a righteous, honest person. You must stay away from this man, if possible. Put distance between yourself and him. Think of his wife and family. You wouldn't want to come between a man and his family, would you?"

"No, Father," she said in a barely audible whisper. "I don't want to be responsible for that."

Her voice was tight as if she hadn't taken a breath in a while; her body was tense.

"Stand true to your convictions and your belief. Ask the Blessed Virgin for guidance, and you won't be led astray. Is there anything else, my child?"

"No, Father."

Sylvia slowly exhaled as she received absolution.

"In the name of Christ our Lord, I absolve you, my child. Say four Our Fathers and ten Hail Marys. Go forth in peace, and sin no more."

Sylvia crossed herself again and genuflected. Father Tom closed the divider. I got out of the booth, and she followed me out of the church. We exchanged glances.

"Well, at least that wasn't weird," I said, as we left through the large wooden doors. Sylvia remained silent. "Feel better now?" I asked.

"Not much. But I know what to do," she said with resolve.

"Oh? What's that?"

"Change churches."

It was the most intelligent thing I'd ever heard her say.

"You know," I said helpfully, "St. Anselm's is pretty nice. The windows aren't creepy at all. And it's not too cold in the winter. And sometimes they have hot chocolate."

She stopped walking and stared at me. "How do you know about St. Anselm's?"

"It's my grandmother-in-law's church."

"Oh." She frowned, looking for her car keys. "What are the priests like at St. Anselm's?"

"Fat and old."

"Well, that's a relief."

It was. I think.

"Or…" she continued slowly and deliberately, "I know," she said with calm resolute, "I've decided."

I stopped rifling through my purse for my car keys and looked at her. She seemed serious.

"You've decided—" I waved my hand that wasn't holding my purse at her, urging her on. "You've decided?" I repeated myself.

"I'm going to become a nun."

"It's funny," I laughed. "I thought you said you were going to become a nun."

She frowned. "I did."

"Oh. Well, when you give your oath of poverty, I'll take those new boots. You won't be needing *them* in the convent."

She didn't seem to appreciate my humor. Sometimes, Sylvia doesn't get me at all. I wasn't worried though. The nun talk was her way of venting. She needed time to heal her wounded heart. Time and maybe a few margaritas.

At home, after the usual Friday night pizza and beer, I took my clipboard out of my bag and sat at the kitchen table. Sylvia's profile hadn't been completed yet. I decided to disregard her nun comment; it was said in the moment, spontaneous. She'd never go through with it. Besides, those things take time. You can't just wake up one day and decide you're going to change your whole life's direction and become a nun. *Or can you?*

What made Sylvia tick? I sat at the table and thought. Stumped. Her life was quiet. She'd never had a boyfriend, so there was no information there. I drummed my pen against the tabletop. She liked chocolate and classical music, babies, old movies, and sunflowers. On paper, Sylvia was seventy-five years old.

There was Father Tom. She liked him. He was handsome, a little older, and kind. I wrote down those attributes. What I knew for sure was: not a lot.

As far as dislikes? Lateness and disorganization—it was a wonder we were friends—loud music, football, and lima beans.

It wasn't much to go on, but it was a start.

"What are you working on?" Javier asked when he spotted me deep in thought working on my Sylvia matrix.

"It's nothing. A project for work."

Javier gave me a strange look. "It's not like you to bring work home, especially on the weekends."

"Okay," I confessed. "It's not actually work-work. It's something I've been working on *at* work."

He gave me another strange look and pulled a beer from the fridge. "All right. I'll leave you alone, but we're ready to start the movie."

It was *Cinderella* night. Matilda's obsession with Disney princesses was full-strength. I'd tried gently explaining to her about how the whole notion of a princess needing to be rescued was a fallacy propagated by a patriarchal society whose real goal was to keep women subjugated, and that the happily-ever-after part might tend to raise her real-life expectations to an unhealthy level, but when I did this, she just looked at me funny and said, "Mommy, I want to watch *Cinderella*."

Disney and unrealistic expectations won again.

"I'll be out in a few minutes," I said to my patient husband.

Frank's profile was last. He liked: women—all shapes, all sizes. That was something to love about Frank. He flirted with everybody. Old ladies giggled like schoolgirls when he told them how lovely they were; young women were drawn to his good looks and charm. I tapped my pen against the edge of the table. What else? Like his son, he was a good cook. He enjoyed long rides on his motorcycle with his friends and was most definitely an alpha male.

Of my group of four, I had two leaders, one follower, and one who wasn't a leader or follower—Ted was his own man.

My basic profiles were complete.

"Babe, the movie's on," Javier called from the living room.

I put my clipboard away, but I wasn't focused on the movie. Instead, the hamster wheel turned slowly. Very slowly. And when I lay in bed, long after Javier was snoring his rhythmic snores, I thought about my subjects, fitting pieces together like a puzzle, turning their different characteristics and attributes over in my head, going over the matrix.

Two alphas; two sensitive types. Two chaste; two of questionable virtue.

Conventional wisdom dictated that couples with like interests should be paired together, which seemed on its face to be sensible, but what about couples like Javier and me? We were nothing alike. I'm spontaneous; Javier is a methodical planner. He's artistic and good with his hands; my one attempt at the womanly art of crochet yielded an elongated baby booty in the shape of an S. He cooked; I burned.

It hit me: opposites attract. I remembered this from Mr. Burnside's Science class. So that made *two* things I learned in my time with him. Opposite charges attract, while like charges repel. If Javier and I, two people not the slightest bit alike, could not only get along but thrive, why wouldn't it work if I set each of my four subjects up with their opposite?

It was my light-bulb moment.

What if every other match I'd made had failed because like charges repel, and they were too much alike? And they certainly found their matches repellant; I'd been told this repeatedly.

It was decided. Alpha Frank would go with follower Sylvia. He was handsome; she was eighteen years younger. She'd certainly find him attractive; he was good-looking and well put together. And she was a *nice* girl, so much nicer than the women he'd been dating where there was always an issue or eccentricity or some type of substance abuse.

The other match scared me a bit. The scary element was: Lisa. She was everything Ted wasn't, *but* she intrigued him. And I'd kept them apart. I felt guilty about that now. It was the whole "playing God" thing that Javier had accused me of. What if they were meant to be together and I'd kept them from finding true love?

But it wasn't too late. I could make things right.

It took me hours to fall asleep; the hamster wheel in my head was spinning too fast for me to drift off. The research portion of my experiment was now complete, my hypothesis created: the notion that opposite couples would be irresistibly attracted to each other.

The next step was conducting the actual experiment itself. The bedside clock read two-forty-five a.m. I lay in bed and mulled it over. All I had to do was get the four together, and the annual combination Cinco de Mayo/Birthday Party was coming up. It was perfect, I simply had to recalibrate and readjust. My original plan had been to bring Sylvia and Ted together at our annual bash. Now plans had changed slightly, but it remained the perfect opportunity.

I had to play it cool though. One thing I'd learned from the totality of my failed matches was that people don't want to know they're being set up. It's as if the minute they get wind of the idea, they put the brakes on, blowing up each perceived fault—even the tiniest little thing—into a giant obstacle. The slightly large nose becomes gargantuan; the little love handle turns into a mountain of blubber. The end result is disaster.

The whole operation would have to be kept on the down low. Top secret.

I rubbed my hands together in silence one last time and slept the comfortable sleep of the happy, well-adjusted matchmaker who knows victory is close at hand. The party was eight weeks away. Plenty of time to plant a few seeds and do a little propagating, propagandizing or hand-holding.

Whatever it took, it was on, baby.

Chapter Twenty-Seven

Sylvia was looking good. Really good. At my nagging—I mean, gentle insistence—she'd given up the clunky granny glasses, trading them in for daily wear contacts.

"Do you know what it's like to be able to put makeup on and actually see what I'm doing?" she said, with much enthusiasm. I didn't, having been blessed with twenty-twenty vision, but I could only imagine what a drag it would be. "It's amazing," she said, visibly excited.

She sat in front of my little vanity table in my bedroom trying out different shades of eye shadow, holding a hand mirror up to her face, examining it. Sylvia was a little inexperienced in the ways of mascara and liner, so I lined the tops of her eyelids with kohl liner and dabbed on a bit of brown shadow.

"Beautiful," I said, appraising my work. "The mascara you're going to have to do yourself."

I didn't want to get that close to her eyes. She took the wand from my hand, immediately poking herself in the eye.

"Ow! My eye!" she wailed.

Ugh. "Wait one second. I'll get a washcloth."

I ran to the bathroom, wet the corner of a washcloth and handed it to her. She snatched it from my hands and held it up to her eye; the whole makeup job was a complete mess.

Baby steps. That was what we needed to do. Baby steps.

"Are you okay?"

"Ow. Yeah." She held the wet cloth up to her eye. "Just let me get this contact out and rinse it."

"Don't worry; it gets better," I told her, trying to cheer her up. I'd been putting makeup on forever, since the seventh grade. It was a skill like anything else. "Maybe we'll leave the mascara for a while," I said as she removed her lens and washed the makeup off at my bathroom sink. "Or you can put the mascara on before you put your contacts in," I suggested.

"But I won't be able to see if I do that," she complained.

It wasn't rocket science. She'd figure it out. It was still March. We had time.

At work, I gave Ted weekly reminders. Subtle. Always subtle. I hovered next to his desk.

"Ted, you'll be joining us for the annual Cinco de Mayo/ Birthday Party, won't you?"

"Oh, um, uh…what day was that again?"

Ted. Not a native Angeleno.

"'Cinco' means five. 'Mayo' is May."

He gave me a look of death.

"Okay, I deserved that. Sorry. I know you weren't brought up steeped in our local traditions. It's May fifth, which falls on a Saturday this year."

"Wow, okay. That's quite a ways off," he said, looking puzzled.

"I know, dear. I'm just letting you know. We'd really like you to be there this year. We always have so much fun," I said in a light and airy way, as if it weren't a matter of life or death whether he showed or not. Even though it totally was. I didn't want to scare him away though.

Ted was my wild card in the whole scenario. Frank and Lisa were annual attendees. Sylvia wouldn't be a problem. She was always home on Saturdays, and I could always physically go over and carry her on my back if she didn't show for some reason. Ted, though, was a completely different story; a man who always went his own way. I'd have to exert my influence on him by using any means necessary. I can be positively diabolical when I choose to be.

"Uh—" he averted his gaze, looking down at his keyboard, then back at me "—is Lisa going to be there?"

Yes.

I suppressed the sudden urge to high-five him and high-five myself, because it would have confused and/or scared him. But I *really* wanted to turn a few cartwheels right there in the office, even in my skirt and heels. *Play it cool. Don't spaz out now, Julia.*

"Lisa? Oh, I guess. Gosh. I hadn't really thought about it. Hmm. Probably."

I studied his face; he concentrated on his blue-and-green plaid tie, which he was now playing with, doing strange things to it, nervously twirling it about, tying then untying it. His right leg was bouncing up and down. He was too transparent.

"Ahem." I cleared my throat; he looked up.

"Um, well, I think I'll—I mean, I'm sure I'll be there."

"I'll send you an e-mail reminder," I said sweetly, the spider to the fly.

"Um, great. That's great, Julia."

I got back to work. Ted sat at his desk, running a hand through his hair. He seemed, although I wasn't completely sure, to be breathing a little heavier.

It was like taking candy from a baby. *Way* too easy.

Lisa was a piece of cake, a sure thing, but I called her from work anyway to cover all bases.

"You're coming to the combination Cinco de Mayo/Birthday Party, aren't you?"

"Why are you asking me this?" she said, her voice suspicious.

"Just making sure."

"Are you drunk? You're not drinking at work now, are you?"

"Very funny. No, just getting my list together. You know how Javier is."

"He's over the top, isn't he? Just a second." She muffled the phone with her hand and spoke to someone in the background. I heard the words, "Stay there. I didn't say you could move yet." There was a man's voice in the background, but I couldn't tell what he was saying.

It was always heartwarming and slightly off-putting listening in on Lisa at work. I spoke loudly into the phone so she'd hear me. "I'll let you go. You sound busy."

"Oh, I can talk for—let's see. Five more minutes."

I didn't ask. Lisa is funny, especially when she's absorbed in business.

"So anything interesting happen with you?" I asked, to be polite.

"Not a thing. My life has been so dull lately," she sighed. "Hold on a sec'." Her voice became muffled again. I heard her say, "Good boy. That's right. Keep stirring."

I couldn't be sure, but it *sounded* like Lisa's client was making her lunch.

"Now add the noodles to the wok and throw in the ginger and garlic," she commanded.

Brilliant.

"What's for lunch," I yelled into the phone.

"Stir-fry."

I pictured Ted with an apron tied around his naked body, whipping up a light lunch for Lisa as she barked commands, riding crop in hand. Then I pushed the thought out of my head with both hands.

"Um, bon appétit. I have to get back to work. We'll talk later."

"See you at the party," Lisa said, sounding all light and happy.

My friends: not dull.

Frank was my only subject left of the four, and I didn't bother checking with him, since it would take a natural disaster or sudden bout of appendicitis to keep him away, and *that* might not even do it. Frank was a sure thing.

The players were in place. Everything was set. It was T-minus fifty-eight days and counting.

Chapter Twenty-Eight

"Babe, you've been quiet," Javier said, his voice tinged with concern. "Is everything all right?"

We were stalking the aisles of Toys "R" Us, shopping for Matilda's birthday while she slept over at her Great-Grandma Terry's house. I'd been in my own matchmaker's private world, living in my head, extra preoccupied with all things romance-related.

"Oh, no, just work stuff."

"Since when do you worry about work stuff?"

He had me there. My work was brain dead; I worked solely on autopilot. I was nervous though, feeling apprehensive, and a little angsty. *What if my plan didn't work?* It would feel like failure as well as an indictment of my whole personal ideal of bringing people together. *And* it would validate everything Javier had ever said; in other words, that I'm a terrible matchmaker.

"It's just the new receptionist isn't really working out, and I was debating whether to tell Roger yet or give her another week."

He shrugged and mumbled something noncommittal like, "Well, whatever you think is best."

Javier rarely gave advice about work; his work issues usually centered on him being afraid to talk to his scary pressman Robert.

"How's Robert these days?" I asked, making conversation while we walked through the board game aisle.

He raised his eyebrows. "Well, he scares the heck out of me, but I can never let him go." I raised my eyebrows back at him, alarmed. He lowered his voice to a whisper and said, "If my body is ever found under suspicious circumstances, you'll know who did it."

I smacked him on the shoulder. "Don't joke about things like that, babe."

He laughed. "I'm kidding. He looks much scarier than he is. Did I tell you he's got a little kitten at home?"

This was a surprise.

"No, you're kidding."

"It was a stray. He found it wandering around the front of his house and gave it a home. He's always talking about her, how cute she is and how she sleeps curled up on his pillow. He named her Pinkie."

A little baby girl kitty named Pinkie. How sweet. It showed that you never could really tell about people. Even the ones who seemed like they might possibly go on a work-related rampage one day.

"Babe, does Robert have a girlfriend?"

Javier stopped dead in his tracks in the middle of the Easy Bake Ovens. "Don't even think about it."

But I did think about it. If scary Robert could find it in his heart to give a little homeless kitty-cat a home, he obviously had the capacity for love. I made a mental note to add Robert to my future to-be-matched list. There had to be a strong woman out there for him. I was thinking female wrestler or gym coach. Or maybe, taking the opposites attract route, someone tiny and shy. I'd have to think on that one.

"I was just wondering about his situation, that's all."

I brushed Javier's skepticism aside, and we trudged on through the miles of square footage in our quest for birthday gifts.

First we looked at two thousand and one different types of Barbie dolls. Next we looked at a dozen pink bicycles, with Javier taking several down from the racks and examining them. We picked a small one with pink tassels on the handlebars and a pink glitter-speckled seat. Matilda was the girliest of girls to be sure.

The playhouse stopped me. I stood there beholding the little Tudor cottage with two square windows and roses painted on the outside with vines crawling upward. It was a house for a princess, if there ever was one. I bent down and wedged my hips through the front opening, instantly reliving kindergarten. Remembering back, I thought about our classroom playhouse with its real-looking kitchen complete with pots, pans, and a stove. Lisa and I would recruit Kenny Davies or Benny Salazar to be our husband. Even then, Lisa was reluctant to play the wife role; she wanted the boys to cook for us *and* wash the dishes.

I waved at Javier through the little window box.

"What are you doing in there?" he asked, looking slightly uncomfortable.

"Can we please get this for me—I mean, for Matilda?"

Javier walked around the playhouse, inspecting it. "This is a nice little setup."

"Wanna come in and play house with me?" I said, flirting with him.

"I do," he said, flirting back. "But there's no way I'm going to fit through that doorway. How in the world did you get in there?"

"Geez, Javier. How big do you think I am?"

He shook his head, muttered something I didn't catch, and continued his walk-around inspection. "Wait for me," I said, squeezing half of myself through the miniature doorway so that the front half of my body was on the outside of the playhouse while the lower half of my body remained inside. Funny thing though, my foot had become wedged in a little indentation that was meant to hold an electrical junction box. I pulled, but my foot would not budge. Javier looked at me, his eyebrows raised, questioning.

I pulled again. Beads of perspiration now dotted my forehead.

"Come on, babe," Javier said. "Stop messing around. We've got more shopping to do."

He was obviously getting impatient and had already started to walk ahead. He didn't see the horror in my eyes, horror from the realization that I couldn't turn my body around to dislodge my foot; it was wedged tight.

I closed my eyes, summoning my strength—and courage, for this was truly an embarrassing predicament, and I knew my loving husband would never let me live it down. "Javier!" I called in a near panic.

He turned around and walked back to me. "What's wrong?"

"I'm stuck."

It was really mean of him to start laughing. I wanted to punch him. But laugh he did, like a big stupid hyena.

"Come on, Javier. I'm really stuck."

"Only you. This could only happen to you." He was shaking with laughter. "Why do I always feel like Ricky Ricardo?"

It wasn't the first time he'd asked that question. A fantasy of me turning *him* over my knee and spanking him played its way through my head.

"Don't just stand there, do something!" I pleaded.

"Okay, calm down. I'll get the manager."

He was leaving me. I wanted to die. A crowd was beginning to form. And a crowd forming is almost *always* a bad sign.

"Why don't they take it apart?" a man said helpfully.

"What if they can't take it apart?" a woman said helpfully.

"Of course they can take it apart. It can't be all in one piece," a third person—an older man with spectacles and a straw hat—chimed in. I liked him. He seemed like he knew what he was talking about.

"Um, do you think you can get me out of here?" I asked him, hopeful.

"I'm sorry. I'd love to help you, young lady, but I don't have any tools with me."

Great.

Two little girls, sisters, walked up with wide eyes and curious expressions.

"What are you doing in that playhouse?" the cute little one with the braids asked.

"It's not for adults," the other one with the ponytail said. I didn't like the way she judged me. She was probably a straight-A student and had never gotten into trouble. Ever.

"I went in to measure it for my backyard and got stuck," I lied.

"Well, you should have had someone smaller go in for you," Ponytail girl said. Again, judgment heavy in her tone.

"Aren't you sweet to be so concerned," I said with a fake smile. "Why don't you go run along. Your parents are probably looking for you."

"No, they're not here. That's my grandpa over there."

The mean girl pointed to the man in the straw hat.

I decided to stare her down. She stared back, unblinking. We said nothing and had a staring war. It was really strange.

Luckily, Javier returned, this time out of breath.

"I had to run all over the whole store to find help."

The help he'd managed to find was a young man who appeared to be all of eighteen, the store's assistant manager. He had that deer-caught-in-headlights look about him. His hamster wheel seemed to be turning slowly. Very slowly.

"Hey, how's it going?" I said to him as he walked up to appraise the situation.

"What's up?" he said with a slight nod.

"Oh, not much. You know how it is when you're stuck in a playhouse."

He didn't even crack a smile. Instead, he walked around the playhouse and conferred with Javier and the man in the straw hat, my would-be geriatric knight in shining armor.

My middle was starting to feel chafed; the doorway was beginning to cut in on the left side of my body where my foot was stuck. I closed my eyes and tried to think of a mantra I could repeat in my head. The hamster wheel in my head turned quickly, but there was no hamster on it. *Please get me out of here*, was all I was able to manage for my internal monologue, repeating it several times.

"You know," Javier said, leaning in, his voice low and playful, "I could leave you here and pick you up in the morning."

"Not nice," I scolded. "Do something, Javier. I'm hungry, I have to go to the bathroom, and I want to go home."

"My poor baby," he said, acting all sweet and concerned now. "We'll get you out in a few minutes. The manager just went to the back for some tools."

Things sounded at least a little promising.

"You know, babe, it is pretty funny," he said with a devil smile. On the face of it, it was funny. Or it would have seemed funny if it were happening to *someone* else.

"Yeah," I said drily. "I might look back on this one day and laugh. But not *this* day."

Javier gave a more genuine smile this time and squeezed my shoulder. "We'll get you out, babe. Don't worry."

I had a vision of a Skil saw cutting through the plywood, which gave me some comfort. The fact that we'd be the proud owners of one jacked-up playhouse brought me less comfort. *But*

with a little paint and a few well-placed screws and duct tape—
one should never underestimate the power of duct tape—it would
be almost like new for our little princess.

I averted my gaze downward, studying the pattern in the
industrial-grade store carpeting as a means of avoiding the
murmuring crowd that now surrounded me. I heard a woman's
voice above the murmurs, the strong mature sound of someone
confident and sure of themselves. The voice of experience.

"It's simple," said the voice. "You just undo this latch
here, and this one here. Hey, you there. Would you mind
taking that end?"

The voice belonged to a middle-aged woman—a strong-
looking lady who wore reading glasses on a chain around her neck
—with short-cropped hair and serious biceps. A match for Robert
maybe? By the uniform, I surmised she was an employee, maybe a
manager. She came over to where I was stuck in the doorway.

"We're going to get you out of there. Just get ready to pull
yourself out when I give the signal."

"You don't know how glad I am to see you. Really glad."

The strong, capable toy store manager gave a brisk nod,
something like a grunt, and turned her attention to business.

"Okay. One and a two…"

They pulled the roof off. The whole thing took about two
seconds, and I was free from my temporary jail, but also suddenly
exposed to the world. I felt very small, and the enthusiastic
clapping of the crowd was humiliating, but I dug down deep
inside of myself and gave the people a quick curtsy.

What else could I do?

While Javier worked out delivery instructions, I found the bathroom. One day maybe we'd share the story of Mom getting stuck in the playhouse. Maybe. Or maybe we'd just keep the whole nasty incident to ourselves. The better alternative, as far as I was concerned, was the latter.

It was T-minus one week and counting. Time to get serious.

Chapter Twenty-Nine

Somewhere in the distance, a bell rang, over and over. Jarring me. It was in a dream. The dream became reality when I opened my eyes at five-thirty a.m., fumbling to hit the snooze bar before rolling over onto my stomach. Javier nudged me gently, whispering in my ear, "Time to get up, babe."

"Umph," I groaned, staggered out of bed, doing my best imitation of a zombie lurching its way toward the kitchen, a few steps behind Javier, who, in a stroke of genius, had set the coffeemaker's timer the night before. Brilliant.

The Hawthorne-Florez combination Cinco de Mayo/ Birthday Party was a go. Me? Not so much. But it was going to be a very long day and night, so I put my big girl panties on, drank two cups of very strong coffee, and geared up as Javier quizzed me, holding his clipboard.

"Tables and chairs?"

"They're being delivered at ten."

"With tablecloths?" he said with arched brow.

"With tablecloths."

"What about the bounce house?" He leaned forward, hovering over me as I fell over to my side on the couch, resting against a throw pillow, trying for two more minutes of sleep. "You did order it, didn't you?" he pressed.

"Of course I did." I was only a little offended by his anal-retentiveness.

"Princess themed?"

"Yes, princess themed."

It was funny; *he* was the one concerned about the princess theme. As far as I was concerned, as long as it held air and allowed the children to bounce themselves silly, all was well.

He made little checks with his pen. It would have been cute except it was too early. And I hate it when he gets all official on me. And I really hate *other* people with clipboards.

"Javier, can we tone it down; relax just a little?" It was only six-fifteen. In the morning. The party was nearly ten hours away.

He sighed a heavy sigh of the long-suffering husband. "Babe, you *know* we've got all kinds of work to do."

I knew. I slapped my own cheeks a couple of times, rolled up my sleeves, and got to work hosing down the back patio.

The weather forecast for the fifth of May: eight-five degrees, clear skies, dropping down to a balmy sixty-eight at night. Practically swimsuit weather. In Los Angeles, this meant skin, glorious skin, in all shapes and sizes, including the unfortunate muffin top or two—something I'll hopefully not be guilty of. Ever. Javier has been instructed to kindly let me know when my belly roll is ever visible above the top of my jeans. It's a public service, really. And I've promised him that I won't be offended. Better knowing than roaming around town a bulging curiosity.

The countdown to the party had begun. The traps had been set, metaphorically speaking. I'd made my mental notes, physical notes, even metaphysical notes. We weren't amateurs; this was strictly a professional operation, and the choreography would play off as it had every year for the past—who knows how many years? —with built-in fail-safes and backups. Not enough food? Frank or one of Javier's uncles had the pizza delivery place on standby. Not enough beer? Impossible. But just in case, there was an emergency stockpile in the garage and two liquor stores within a five-minute drive. Two piñatas were filled with mini-Snickers bars, Tootsie Pops, and Lemonheads—one for the girls, and one for the boys. A spare cake sat in the garage refrigerator. The barbecues were lined up and ready to go, with a spare tank of propane in reserve.

All systems go.

Somewhere around midafternoon, the bikers descended as if they'd been dropped from Heaven—large bundles with rough beards and voices gruff from years of smoking and living hard. The rumble of twenty Harleys pulling up at once made the entire house shake slightly. Javier's uncles had arrived.

Javier, clipboard in hand, directed them to their stations with much authority.

"Rocky, you're in charge of the bar. Puff, you get the bounce house. Uncle Leo, I need you to help with the barbecues." And so it went, like clockwork.

Uncle Leo then divided the barbecue duty. Uncle Joey would do the hotdogs and buns, Big Bob would take hamburgers, and Leo himself would cover the carne asada and tortillas.

Everything was in place and prepared for, except for the surprises. There were a few of those.

As I balanced on the third step of the ladder, my body contorted, taping an end of crinkled-up purple crepe streamer to one of the wooden crossbeams under the patio, I heard a man's throat clearing. It was Frank. I nearly fell off the ladder from the sudden shock of his appearance.

"Can I give you a hand," he offered sweetly. I gasped. It was one of those things you might expect to see in an alternate universe where everything was the same but slightly askew, like where there'd exist another Julia Hawthorne-Florez, but instead of short, blonde hair, that Julia would have long, dark hair and wear lederhosen. Or something like that. I don't know. I mean, it *could* happen.

In this particular version of an alternate universe, my father-in-law had morphed into an almost average, clean-cut middle-aged man. The handlebar mustache and beard? Gone. The usual uniform of pressed Levi's, T-shirt, bandanna, and motorcycle boots? Gone.

"Where is my father-in-law?" I demanded. "And what have you done with him?"

He laughed. "Can't a man change things up a little? I mean, my granddaughter only turns six once."

"Wait one second," I said, scrambling down from the ladder to give him a proper greeting. We exchanged cheek kisses. "Let me get a look at you."

I stepped back a step so I could take him in, in all of his newly minted handsomeness. It was nothing short of a combination Cinco de Mayo/Birthday Party miracle: my father-in-law was wearing a white *polo* shirt, khaki slacks, and loafers. *Penny* loafers complete with pennies tucked carefully inside. He beamed; I almost fell over from the shock. Plus, I was a little light-headed from getting up and down the ladder around twenty million times to hang the stupid streamers. *And* from growling at Javier's insistence on having the backyard well decorated. Frank had taken my little suggestions to heart. And then some.

It was the magic of Cinco de Mayo; it had to be. That was the only plausible explanation I could come up with for his transformation and willingness to take my makeover suggestions.

I called out to Javier, who was lugging bags of ice from the garage for the coolers. "Babe, look at your dad."

Javier slammed the fifty-pound bag down on the concrete to free his hands and walked over next to his father, looking him up and down, stunned.

"Well, what do you think?" Frank asked, beaming.

Javier shook his head, searching for words. "If I were a cynical man, which I'm not—"

I snorted. I couldn't help it. Javier shot me a dirty look.

"As I was saying, Ms. *Florez*, if I were a cynical man, I'd say it's to impress a woman."

"Please, *mijo*. You *really* think I'm using my granddaughter's birthday party to cruise for chicks?" Frank asked, pretending to be wounded.

"I said 'if.' You look great, Pop. You really do," Javier said, giving Frank a slap on the back, then adding, "Just wait till the boys get a look at you."

"I'm not looking forward to that," Frank said, looking a bit apprehensive. The boys would give him a load of crap; that was a certainty. But I was dancing on the inside. If Frank's old biker gang didn't like it—too bad for them.

"I'm impressed, Frank," I said. "You look *really* good. Just let me get my suitcase, and we'll blow this taco stand. I've been waiting for an opportunity to escape my humdrum life, and here it is."

Javier was not amused, shot me another dirty look, and put his father to work unloading ice into his system of coolers and bartending apparatuses. My husband is a true party professional. I've often thought he should go into the catering business.

I went back to hanging streamers, inwardly humming, resisting the impulse to rub my hands together in delight, and listened as "the boys" had their fun, making rude comments about Frank's new look. I heard the word "pussy" as in, "Frank, you big pussy," at least five times. I shook my head in disgust. Philistines. And of all people to talk—Uncle Puff and Big Bob were both in serious need of makeovers. They were *next* on my list.

As I hung balloons to be suspended from the patio, I thought about Sylvia and the dress I'd helped her pick out for the party, hoping she'd actually wear it. I was crossing my fingers that she wouldn't revert to her old ways of blousy, shapeless clothing best left to the elderly.

Things were definitely looking up. I felt cautious optimism.

Around four, guests began filtering in. Matilda was by this point running in circles, fueled by newly turned six-year-old energy, and I hadn't actually spoken to my husband since the bouncer delivery men had arrived.

I greeted kids, parents, conducted hostess duties, running in several directions at once, while Javier organized the kids into a group for a game of Simon Says. At four-thirty, he called over to me, "Babe, the Cruzes are here."

I smoothed my hair behind my ear and went to greet them.

The Cruzes—all four of them—made their way around the side gate into the backyard. As I greeted each one, Frank appeared as if out of nowhere, introducing himself before I could.

"Hello, I'm Frank, Matilda's grandfather." He held out his hand to Sylvia's father Antonio first.

"*Mucho gusto,*" Antonio said, shaking Frank's hand warmly. "This is my wife Ofelia, my son Raul, and my daughter Sylvia."

Frank gave Ofelia a polite peck on the cheek, shook hands with Raul, and stopped when he got to Sylvia, who lowered her gaze, self-conscious as usual. I noticed the corners of her mouth were slightly turned up.

Frank, you dog, you.

I found the whole scene to be extremely interesting and tried my best to ignore Javier's Uncle Puff, who was waving at me, trying to get my attention. There was something going on with the bounce house. I waved back, trying to wave him off, so I could watch the scene playing out before me.

My father-in-law oozed charm. Sylvia stood before him, a vision. She really was. She'd been practicing with her hair and makeup and had ditched the clunky glasses. The contacts had turned out to be a bust, but her new frames were lighter and modern. Her sundress, white with a red floral pattern, wasn't exactly sexy, more sweet. She was perfect.

I hovered nearby, straightening one of the food tables, organizing the plastic knives and forks for the tenth time, and watched as Frank paused, looking directly into Sylvia's eyes, and took her outstretched hand. He gently brought it up to his mouth and kissed it, lightly grazing the skin. "It's a pleasure to meet you."

I wished I had a bowl of popcorn. And time to watch.

Sylvia smiled shyly, and I saw something in her parents' eyes, something like…relief? Ofelia seemed to perk up as if she were considering the possibilities of the situation. Like maybe all of her daily prayers had *finally* been answered?

"Have we met before?" Sylvia asked in a quiet, almost indiscernible, voice. Luckily, my hearing is doglike in its acuity.

"No, I don't think so. Surely I would have remembered meeting someone as beautiful as you."

Frank, you dog, you.

My eyes may have been playing tricks on me, but I could have sworn that I saw Ofelia look up to the sky, giving quick thanks.

I inserted myself back into the scene. "Frank, would you show our friends to a table, help get them situated? It seems that I have a situation to take care of."

I wasn't lying. The bounce house seemed to be going south.

He smiled at me. "Of course, of course. Right this way. There's a table in the corner, not too close to the barbecue, so you won't get smoke in your eyes…"

I watched for a few moments as he ushered the four of them to a table, pulling a chair out for Ofelia, acting the perfect gentleman. He next pulled a chair away from the table for Sylvia and offered to get their drinks.

It could have been my imagination, but the two seemed to be making eyes at each other. I wanted to pinch myself.

Two down, two to go.

By five o'clock, the backyard was full of partygoers. Lisa still hadn't arrived, nor had Ted, but I kept it together, glancing at my watch every few seconds. Things would turn out. There was plenty of time. I repeated this mantra to myself: everything will work out.

I was stationed next to the CD player as Javier led the children over to a circle of chairs for a game. It was like herding a group of rowdy cats with short attention spans.

"Ready kids? You pass the potato while Julia plays the music. When the music stops, whoever has the potato in their hands is out."

He gave me a signal to turn the music on. I pushed the button on the player. "This old man, he played one, he played knickknack on my thumb," issued forth, and the children passed the spud with many giggles and gleeful screams. Someone tapped my shoulder.

"Where's the gin?"

It was Lisa dressed for the clubs in a short black leather skirt and matching bustier.

"A bustier? Really?"

"Hey, this was a regular party for adults before the kid came along. Not my problem."

"It's fine. We'll keep you in that half of the yard." I pointed toward the bar and Javier's uncles. The kids were still passing the potato around; Javier was giving me a meaningful look.

"Oh. Sorry." I hit the Stop button and Matilda's little friend Angel was stuck holding the potato, looking depressed. Poor Angel.

Lisa, who is half evil, took a look at Angel's face, threw her head back and laughed her wicked laugh.

"Life's hard," she said, and she was off, collecting kisses from Javier's uncles. Our annual Combination Cinco de Mayo/Birthday Party was starting to get a little strange with the colliding of the two worlds.

I glanced at my watch; it was five-thirty. I was starting to get nervous.

Where was Ted?

Chapter Thirty

"Crap."

I'd been scanning the party the way a person who's hosting a large gathering does and noticed that the bouncer was starting to list to one side again. The dumb thing had been a pain in my backside all party long. Too many children jumping in one area were throwing off the center of gravity. A vision of it coming free from its moorings, being carried by the wind and landing on the roof of Doris's house next door flitted through my brain. I'd seen something like that on the news once. Luckily, the winds weren't too high.

Javier's Uncle Puff—so named because in spite of his four-hundred-plus-pound frame, he moved with the grace of a ballerina—gave me a warning glance. "Want me to take care of that?" he said in his gruff voice.

"Would you, Puff?"

He was all business as he ordered all of the little children to come out so he could do a safety inspection and walk-around. Again, it was like herding cats, but these cats listened to the scary giant with their wide-eyes and innocent faces.

"All right, kids. We're going to do this by size. Three- to five-year-olds only now."

He had them lining up by age. It was cute and enormously complicated as he arranged them in groups by age and weight.

"Thanks, Puff. You're a doll."

He grunted and let the first group back into the bounce house, which was no longer pulling to the left.

A glance at my watch revealed that it was almost time for cake and an assessment of the overall situation. I hadn't seen Javier for the longest time. Frank and Sylvia were laughing and talking. I smiled at the two of them and watched with interest as my brother Chris, who'd arrived with my parents, was sitting next to Sylvia's brother Raul. Then I did a double take when I walked closer to the table and spotted Raul with a set of tarot cards giving Chris an impromptu reading.

Very interesting.

I hovered near them, listening to Raul explain to my brother the priest why the sun card was a good omen since it signified harmony, happiness and solid relationships. Chris looked over at me hopefully; I gave him a subtle thumb's up that only he could see.

Raul was a good-looking—if quiet—guy, like Chris. I watched them for a moment, my body tingling with new energy. It was too soon to congratulate myself, but not too soon to think about them and ponder the situation. I smiled to myself, proud of this unplanned pairing.

"Julia, I'm so sorry I'm late."

I looked up from my self-congratulating to see Ted approaching.

"Ted!"

He was dressed for a backyard party in jeans, a Hawaiian shirt, and sunglasses. His hair was lightly tousled. He was relaxed and casual, not his usual buttoned-up self. In a strange twist, he'd arrived wearing the clothes my father-in-law would normally wear, and Frank was dressed like preppie Ted. *Very* strange.

"I'm sorry. I got caught in traffic."

"No need to apologize. I'm just glad you're here. Let me get you a plate of food, and something to—"

"Mm-hmm. It's nice to see you too…" He trailed off, his attention elsewhere. I turned to see where he was looking, and where he was looking was Lisa.

It was almost too easy. I mentally high-fived myself; the hamster wheel in my brain was spinning faster than it ever had, threatening to come off its rails.

"Ted, it's good to see you again," Lisa purred, kissing him on the cheek but letting her lips linger a half second too long.

"Lisa. Um, it's, uh, good to—"

"Why don't you get us something to drink?" Her voice was authoritative; he was off in a shot.

"Well done," I said. "Does it always work like that for you?"

"Not always. Nine times out of ten though."

She smiled, very pleased with herself. So was I. We chatted until Ted returned with the drinks, looking flushed and excited.

"Uh, is a screwdriver okay?" he asked.

Lisa turned to me, her eyebrow arched.

"Don't," I said.

She smirked. Pure evil. Oh, it was too perfect. Lisa was devouring Ted with her eyes; he was caught in her tractor beam, helpless, as she pulled him in. I felt myself starting to perspire just a little at the top of my forehead from the heat they were generating.

"Well," I said, clearing my throat, "I'll just leave you two alone then."

Things were moving right along. The cells in my body were all atwitter, vibrating with excitement. I was *almost* beside myself, but there was still work to be done. No time to celebrate. Yet.

By eight-thirty, the birthday cake was sliced; the piñatas were bashed to bits; presents were opened. The birthday party portion of the evening had been a success. We said goodbye to Matilda's school friends, and Javier handed each child their own princess gift bag stuffed with candy and little toys.

With the children's party over, the adult portion was just getting started. The music played, and the paper lanterns twinkled, hanging from the bottlebrush trees. Javier grabbed me by the arm, pulling me close for a dance under the stars. We swayed to the music, his hand firm on the small of my back. He twirled me around and dipped me, his face an inch from mine— so close, I could feel his breath.

"Kiss me," I said.

We kissed with heat that made me want to steal away with him for a few minutes, then he returned me to an upright position, slightly light-headed. He spoke in a low voice, his lips pressed against my ear. "Interesting party. I just saw my father walk out with Sylvia and her parents."

"Hmm. What do you know?" I said. "That *is* interesting."

He stopped dancing and stared at me, watching my face closely, softly shaking his head. I could tell he was onto me. "You don't seem too surprised," he said calmly.

"Well, if you think *that's* interesting, wait until you hear the rest of the story."

He was intrigued; I could tell.

"I give up. What's the rest of the story?"

I smiled my great big smile of victory and watched as Lisa and Ted snuck away behind Javier's back. She led; he followed.

"The rest of the story I guess we'll have to find out tomorrow," I said.

It was true. The rest of the story was yet to come. I still needed to analyze the results and draw conclusions, using my scientific method. But the signs so far pointed to a highly successful outcome.

By ten-forty-five, we'd said our last goodbyes. I hugged bikers, retrieved purses from the spare room, and performed all other hostly duties.

"Great party, you guys." Chris gave me a light peck on the cheek; his face was positively glowing. "Raul's taking me to a little jazz club nearby for a nightcap." He looked over at his new friend. "Are you ready?"

"Let's go," Raul said in his quiet way.

Raul turned to Javier and me. "Lovely party, Julia, Javier," he said in his clipped, proper way of speaking. He tucked his sport coat under his arm and the two men left, walking very close together.

As soon as they were out of earshot, Javier and I both spoke at once.

"Do you think—" I said.

"What was that—"

"I have no idea," was all I could manage.

Our questions were left unanswered. Javier shook his head and said simply, "I have no words. I don't know what to think anymore."

Neither did I.

The two of us sat, exhausted, on the living room couch, wine glasses in hand. Matilda was sprawled out, fast asleep, amidst her haul of presents.

The evening's magic had me feeling slightly off balance though. The thought of my brother and Sylvia's brother had me feeling a little befuddled. I turned to my husband and said, "Javier, tell me something."

"Yes?"

"Is the Earth still spinning in the sky? And is there still one sun in the sky? One moon? Am I still Julia from Silver Lake?"

Javier looked at me, thought for a moment, and answered. "Yes, the Earth, as far as I know, is still spinning. And, the last time I looked, there was still one sun in the sky, one moon. And yes, you are still Julia Hawthorne-Florez of Silver Lake."

"Okay. Just checking."

He was quiet for another moment and said softly, "But I've been thinking…"

"Have you now? What about?"

"I've been thinking that you may possibly be the world's greatest matchmaker."

"Come on. Don't tease me."

"No, I'm serious." He looked into my eyes, trying to impress his words upon me. "For the first time that I can remember, my dad seems to be interested in a *real* woman, someone he might be able to have an actual adult relationship with." He shook his head, pursing his lips. "And Ted. My God. Ted is probably having sex for the first time in his life. Right now as we speak." He laughed, shaking his head in disbelief.

That was a good thought. I felt myself getting all tingly inside again, imagining the possibilities and thinking about the wonder of newfound love. My inner romantic was turning cartwheels; I wanted to pinch myself to see if it were all real.

"And your brother," he continued, "Good Lord. If he and Raul hit it off, that's two more people—two more lost souls—who've found each other. It's crazy. Completely crazy. It's almost as if you'd planned the whole thing."

He stared at me. Waiting.

I held my hands, palm sides up, in the air and gave a little shrug of the shoulders. I had planned at least some of it, but there was more to it than that. There were other factors at work—things that I didn't understand. Something magical had happened, and the two of us sat quietly for a moment, absorbing the wonder of it all.

Then Javier picked Matilda up and carried her off to bed. I followed him down the hall and kissed her on the cheek as she slept peacefully. I could almost see the halo floating above her angelic head.

We went into our bedroom, and I sat down, beyond exhausted, on the edge of the bed. I pulled my sundress up over my head and felt Javier's warm hands on my stomach. He's never been able to resist the soft pooch of my belly. He kissed my skin, pulling me over to his side of the bed.

"After eight years, I still love kissing you," I said, feeling the electricity between us as I always did.

"Eight years to the day," he said.

He hadn't forgotten. It was the eighth anniversary of the first time we'd met, and we celebrated accordingly. The spark was still there.

Chapter Thirty-One

Javier and I spent the morning after the party cleaning up:
picking up bottles and cans, putting them in the recycling bin,
washing dishes, organizing. By early afternoon, my curiosity had
gotten the best of me. No phone calls; no missed calls. And I'd
checked my cell phone, checked our landline, repeatedly.

There is perhaps nothing as annoying as being in desperate
want of information and not getting it. I wasn't worried about
Sylvia. I knew not a whole lot could have happened with her
parents in such close range; they were built-in chaperones. It was
Ted I felt so anxious about. It was almost a sure thing that he had
had no significant experience with women. I wasn't positive about
this; even I have my limits and had never been able to bring
myself to ask him whether he was a virgin. The word itself gives
me the serious heebies. But I had my doubts. Or if he *had*
previously been with a woman, it was probably one of those
awkward clumsy encounters best left forgotten.

Poor Ted. If he only knew what went on in my tattered brain.

Lisa. She could literally eat him alive. Maybe Ted was dead.
Okay, my imagination was running a bit ahead of me on that one.
I smacked myself in the head, paced, and checked my phone

another fifty times. Then I gave in and called Ted's cell. It rang; Lisa answered.

"Hello, Ted's cell phone," she purred.

"Where's Ted? And what have you done with him?"

Lisa laughed. It was the laugh of the evil jungle cat that's successfully cornered the poor wildebeest and is now toying with him.

"He's a little tied up right now."

Oh, the visions. The neurons in my brain were firing all at once. The hamster wheel turned furiously, threatening to come off its rails again.

"You didn't. Tell me you didn't."

"Oh, I *did*."

Lisa held the phone away from her face and called out, "How are you doing, Ted?"

I heard a muffled voice in the background, and then she came back on the line.

"Ted says to tell you hello."

Ted, you dog!

"Don't worry. They're soft restraints," Lisa offered as a way to mitigate the situation. "He could get away if he *really* wanted to. I don't think he wants to though," she said sounding content and satisfied about the whole thing.

I could just picture her in a black latex bodysuit, stiletto heels, bullwhip in hand. And the swing. I was dying to know his reaction when he saw it hanging there, suspended from the ceiling. My cheeks felt hot just thinking about Ted and "the swing."

"Well, don't hurt him. Please."

"Julia, I'm offended that you'd say such a thing." She sounded wounded. "What I do doesn't hurt."

It was true; Lisa was a complete professional. She used safe words and everything. I made a mental note to ask her later what their safe word had been. Also, what Ted had to say about her St. Andrew's Cross with spanking bench.

"Oh, I know. It's just…he's so innocent."

"Not anymore." Lisa laughed again. She cracked herself up with that. "Listen, Julia, I've never purposely hurt anyone in my life, and I don't intend to now."

That was also true. Lisa loved men; she loved sex. There was something else: the tone in her voice was different. For all of the time I'd known her, which was since the age of five, and for maybe the first time since we'd been friends, I heard something approaching softness in her voice as she spoke about Ted.

"I'm keeping this one. I mean, I think he could be the one," she said with the slightest hint of vulnerability in her voice, and I believed her.

It was stupendous. Miraculous. And unbelievable. All three.

"Well—" I paused, trying to formulate a thought "—I'm happy for you both. We'll talk later."

I sat down on the chair in the kitchen, woozy, struggling to process what I'd heard. Everything was topsy-turvy, as if the Earth's poles had suddenly reversed and the world was now spinning in the opposite direction. Even though I'd planned and schemed, I hadn't fully prepared myself for success.

Chapter Thirty-Two

Javier was heating left over tortillas and carne asada as I mashed avocados for fresh guacamole when the doorbell rang.

Javier looked at me. "Expecting anyone?"

I shrugged. "No, but maybe we need to set an extra plate."

It was Frank, on our doorstep.

"Didn't we just see you last night?" I said, teasing. "Come in."

He looked all refreshed and energetic with a great big smile on his face. "Just for a minute. I've got dinner plans."

"Oh?"

"Antonio invited me over to Sunday dinner," he said with a smile.

Frank, you dog.

I couldn't help myself; I hugged him, squeezing him extra tight.

"What was that for?" he said, after I released him.

"Nothing. Nothing at all," I lied. I felt like I had swallowed a whole rainbow, I was so happy.

Javier came out of the kitchen to greet his father, wiping his hands on a dish towel.

"Are you joining us for dinner, Pop?"

Frank looked at me; I remained silent. My mouth was frozen in a ridiculous smile.

"No, *mijo*," he said quietly. "I'm eating dinner with your neighbors."

Javier looked at me, open mouthed, wiped his hand on the towel, and went back into the kitchen muttering, "I don't know anything anymore."

"Frank," I said when my power of speech returned, "I'm happy for you. I really am."

"Well, we'll see where it goes." He gave a little laugh. "I can't remember the last time I was invited to a woman's house for Sunday dinner by her parents." He shook his head. "Actually, I don't think I *ever* have been."

I gave him a kiss on the cheek for luck and walked him out.

The world was a wonderful place of puffy hearts and puffy clouds. Anything was possible, now that love had been found.

As soon as I closed the door behind Frank, I grabbed the phone to call Sylvia, attempting to play it cool.

"Hey, Sylvia. How are you today?"

"Oh, Julia! I meant to call you—"

I detected a hint of breathlessness in her voice.

"So…expecting anyone for dinner?" I asked casually.

"Julia! Oh, my God! I was going to tell you everything later—I didn't want to jinx things—but *Frank's* coming over for dinner."

"What the heck?"

"I know. My *father* invited him."

"Well, that sounds serious. Are we picking out the china yet?"

She laughed. "Come on. Let's be serious." She sighed a giddy sigh of a woman with a serious crush. "I really like him though. I mean, really really."

"Really?"

She laughed again. "I don't know. It's the craziest thing, but we hit it off. I'm so comfortable with him. Anyway, I've gotta go—the doorbell just rang." She let out a small squeal. "I'll call you later."

Father Tom was now apparently a distant memory. It was almost too much to process. I hugged myself and let out my own little squee of joy.

The world was all fluffy bunnies and wonder, lollipops and marshmallows. The world seemed to have suddenly turned into a real-life version of Matilda's Candy Land game. And that's just the way I like it.

Chapter Thirty-Three

What is matchmaking? It's the simple act of bringing two people together, which is what I do. Sometimes people find love on their own, but sometimes all they need is a little push in the right direction. And while I admit I don't know everything there is to know about love—there are too many variables and intangibles to really get a grasp on it all—what I do know is that Sylvia and Frank were now happy; Ted and Lisa were also happy; Raul and Chris were on their way to happy, and that, in turn, makes *me* very happy.

In the end, I learned a few things. My quiet and shy friend Ted, as it turned out, didn't want to be with a nice wholesome girl. What he really desired was a strong alpha woman to lead him around and give him orders. It just goes to show, you can never tell with the quiet ones. Or, to trot out an old cliché, still waters run deep. Better yet, still waters like to be spanked. And Lisa, the person I've known longer than anyone besides my family, was finally happy in a traditional—for her—long-term monogamous relationship.

I also learned that the magic of Cinco de Mayo is real.

Javier still says God laughs at me, but I say he laughs *with* me. And while my matchmaking skills may be up for debate, I decided to follow my passion and made the formal move and accepted my dream job as head office administrator to Lady Yvette, professional matchmaker. She's promised to teach me all of the ins and outs of the matchmaking business. Her company, located in Beverly Hills, is called No More Lonely People. I couldn't have come up with a better name myself.

Who's laughing *now*, Javier?

 . . .

Acknowledgments

There are a few people I'd like to acknowledge. First, I'd like to thank my editor, Rory Olsen, for her help and for being so delightful to work with. Thank you to my partner in love and life, Steven, for the beautiful cover and interior book design. I probably wouldn't have written this book if it weren't for his encouragement as well as the cheering on of my good friend Melinda. Both of them asked for more of Julia's adventures. Also, extra thanks to Steve for putting up with me during the whole writing/publishing process. A special thank you goes out to Laura Goodman who patiently read and re-read my work in progress, making helpful suggestions and giving gentle critiques.

Thank you to my mother Marian and my mother-in-law Sue for your constant love and support. Thank you to my sisters Mary, Kathy, and Jenny for being yourselves.

Lastly, I want to thank those individuals out there in the world who believe in love. To borrow a piece of a quote from John Lennon: "love is the answer." I believe that it is. Let's all love one another.

About the Author

California girl Margaret Lesh lives with her husband and son in a quiet suburb near Los Angeles. She writes middle grade, young adult, and women's fiction. When she's not writing, she's thinking about baked goods, especially donuts, far too often. She believes tacos are magic.

- **Visit her website:** www.margaretlesh.com

- **Amazon:** www.amazon.com/Margaret-Lesh/e/B009M7NUVI/ ref=ntt_athr_dp_pel_1

- **Blog:** storyrhyme.com/jcsblog

- **Twitter:** @MargaretLesh

- **Facebook:** facebook.com/pages/Margaret-Lesh-Author-Page/ 275437492511550